THE MODESTY CURE

EMILY TILTON

Published by Stormy Night Publications and Design, LLC.
www.StormyNightPublications.com

Cover design by Korey Mae Johnson
www.koreymaejohnson.com

Images by Period Images, 123RF/Phaisarn Wongkulchata, and
123R/David Martyn Hughes

1st Print Edition. October 2016

ISBN-13: 978-1539375623

ISBN-10: 1539375625

CHAPTER ONE

Eighteen-year-old Amanda Eaker wished her parents had never come to Renford-on-Tees. Nowhere else, as far as she could determine, could a man forty years a girl's senior claim her as his bride. But Mr. George Charlton, a gentleman farmer, had chosen Amanda, and Lord Rider, the squire of Renford-on-Tees, had sent his steward to tell Mr. and Mrs. Eaker that Amanda would become Mrs. George Charlton in a fortnight's time.

"The squire bids me tell you that your daughter is to be instructed above all in the matter of the proper obedience of a young bride in the marriage bed," Amanda heard the steward say. She had taken a stand behind the door to the front parlor, so she could hear the terrible news. "I trust I need be no more explicit than that. Miss Eaker must however be made aware that Mr. Charlton plans to exercise his conjugal rights on a daily basis, and that the squire— being an old friend of Mr. Charlton—has told him that he should not hesitate to exercise them in any fashion he chooses, including..."

Here the steward's voice fell too low for Amanda, whose face now glowed as hot as the sun, to hear. But her mother exclaimed, "No! Begging your pardon, sir, but he mustn't!

1

'Tis unnatural—and unlawful!"

"Must I remind you, Mrs. Eaker, that the squire is our magistrate and I his judicial clerk?"

"We shall leave the county," her father said resolutely.

"I think you would find that an extremely unwise step, Mr. Eaker. Your mortgage is of course held by the squire, and you would go forth penniless. Nor would the squire recommend you as tenants, when others of his class enquired. I shall bid you good day. Mr. Charlton will be here to make his proposal this evening. Please have Miss Eaker ready to meet with him, and to give an affirmative answer with no missishness on the one hand or coquetry on the other."

At the thought of those two poles of the miss and the coquette, Amanda's face burned even hotter, and she ran from the house and hid in her favorite grove of trees, which separated her family's farm from the park of Rider Hall. She heard her parents calling for her, but she couldn't bear to face the news—the same awful news that had come to her friend Jane Sweetser two months before, when the squire had 'encouraged' Mr. Penny, a man of fifty—younger than Mr. Charlton but equally a widower and an old friend of the squire's—to propose to Jane.

Tearfully, knowing she must accept him for her family's sake, Jane had gone to the altar. She had hoped that Mr. Penny would prove more tender to her after he had wed his young bride than he had during his brusque courtship of her. But what Jane told Amanda about her married life made Amanda feel she could never bear to be Mrs. George Charlton—that she must now run away, even if she should be ruined that way.

Jane had to serve Mr. Penny's lusts in his bed every night and every morning, and sometimes during the day as well. She told Amanda, who had been innocent of what the vicar called *the ways of the flesh* and *carnality*, what it meant to have a husband—what it meant that a girl's husband had conjugal rights.

If Jane refused Mr. Penny those conjugal rights, as she had tried to do at first, he strapped her down over a trestle and caned her until she screamed that he might do as he wished. Then, Jane said, with a terrible shudder and a hot blush, he did—right over the trestle where he had just caned her. Amanda thought that what Jane had said about the unnatural way Mr. Penny had taken her after that caning, how he had entered along a passage too narrow for Jane's comfort while she cried out in shame, must refer to the same thing Lord Rider's steward had intimated to Mr. and Mrs. Eaker—the unnatural, unlawful thing Mr. Charlton planned to enforce upon Amanda herself. Jane said that Mr. Penny often enjoyed her that way now, and said that her bottom would have to grow accustomed to him because he did not intend to have a large family.

Nor did that make the worst thing, it seemed, for Mr. Penny made Jane kneel before him, naked, every day. He unbuttoned his breeches, and trained her to give him his way inside her mouth as well. Jane said the hardest part came when Mr. Penny took hold of her head and thrust his virility in and out until he shot what he called his seed down her throat and made her swallow it, saying that this practice, too, would prevent the necessity of feeding a gaggle of children.

Could she hope that Mr. Charlton would be a different sort of man from Mr. Penny? For a few moments in the grove Amanda tried to raise her hopes in that direction. All she knew of Mr. Charlton, really, was that he was wealthy. Mr. Penny, too, had a tidy fortune, but Amanda didn't think he had prospered to the same degree as the older man—the man who planned to make a proposal of marriage to Amanda this evening.

But had not the steward said to her parents that Amanda must expect exactly the same sort of conduct from her suitor that Jane now must endure from Mr. Penny? The tears trickled freely down Amanda's cheeks, and she brushed them angrily away. She would set out from here right now. She had enough education to read and write respectably, thanks to Mrs. Bates, the village schoolmistress. She had the clothes and linen upon her back, which she supposed might secure her a place at least as a scullery maid—for Amanda could see clearly she would have no references, and a girl with no references couldn't aspire to the post of parlor maid. She would endeavor to raise her station from there, and her parents, not knowing where she had gone, would probably take no blame from the squire. Perhaps they would remove as soon as they might from Renford-on-Tees, and they could be reunited. It could not be her duty, though, to accept Mr. George Charlton.

"I say, are you all right?" said a masculine voice behind her, from the other side of the grove—the park side.

Amanda, who had sat down upon the dry leaves from the oaks, turned to see a young man of about thirty, in the day dress of a gentleman—a smart buff-colored suit, with a gleaming white collar and a red cravat—coming toward her through the trees. Had he heard her, when she had sobbed a bit just a few moments before? Could he see that her eyes were rimmed in red?

She looked down at her faded blue work dress and the unstarched apron that covered it. A farmer's daughter—and decidedly not a *gentleman* farmer's daughter. Mrs. Bates had warned the girls sternly about just this sort of occurrence, hadn't she? How the young gentlemen who stayed at houses like Rider Hall would sometimes make a sport of seeking out farmers' daughters for the purpose of *dallying* with them. How only *coquettes* would stay to *dally*, if they saw a young gentleman approaching.

Amanda stood and turned to flee back to her house where proposal or no, she had chores to do. But the confused impressions of the steward's visit, of the idea that a man past fifty would soon be in her parlor, making it clear to her under the guise of a proposal that he intended to enjoy her just as Amanda supposed a young man likes to dally with a coquette, seemed to root her to the ground of the little grove.

Behind the screen of a marriage that represented none of the tender affection that should accompany that most holy of unions, Mr. Charlton meant to have his own kind of dalliance, without even the sweet words Mrs. Bates had warned the village girls young gentlemen would use to encourage the coquettish vice that lived inside every girl. Shouldn't Amanda feel herself free, then, to hear such sweet words once, if she were never to have the chance again?

And if she should decide to flee, after all? Perhaps, she suddenly thought—though in a very vague way—this young gentleman would help her get away!

She turned back to him, to see that he had approached now within a few yards of her. He moved hesitantly, as if worried that she might bound away from him like a fawn and be gone among the thickets. He had a handsome, firm-jawed face, graced with elegant whiskers. His hair was of a chestnut hue, and he had hazel eyes so light they seemed to glow in the morning sun that filtered through the branches.

The way he seemed to stalk her, like a deer, evoked in Amanda's breast two countervailing and yet somehow also harmonizing instincts: to bound away indeed—or, since a girl cannot bound as well as a fawn, at least to take to her heels the way Mrs. Bates would advise—and to giggle. Perhaps, the wild thought came to her, she could giggle and then run, then stop and giggle some more. She supposed she had always imagined dryads behaved that way.

Instead of either the running or the laughter, though, Amanda raised her hands in front of her apron, clasping them together in what she thought might perhaps look like a prayerful posture, though she had not intended it as such. The young man stopped, looking into her eyes. Then, after a long moment of silence in which upon Amanda's side at least nothing at all occurred of a cognitive nature but rather the mere gathering of impressions—the smell of leaves, the warmth of the dappled sunlight, the appearance of true manly beauty before Amanda's eyes for the very first time—

he repeated his question.

"Are you all right, Miss...?"

Clever man, Amanda thought, to end his sweet words with that ellipsis into which she could not but drop her name.

"Eaker," she said simply, because she could think of nothing else in the world to say. "I am... yes, I am all right."

"But surely you've been weeping, Miss Eaker," he said, his eyes widening a little. Then they widened still more, and he continued, "But I must... yes, I..." The very slightest red tinge came upon his face then, but it disappeared so quickly that Amanda could not feel sure she had seen it. "My name is James Coventry. I'm a school chum of the squire's son."

Had he meant to say something more? Amanda felt quite sure he had, as she considered, and she felt just as sure that something about her own name had caused his momentary surprise.

"Of Mr. John Rider?" she asked, in order that no awkward silence fall between them. John had matriculated to Oxford the previous autumn.

"No, of Mr. Philip Rider."

Amanda nodded, feeling obscurely that this commonplace conversation, though it seemed not to involve sweet words of blandishment, had nevertheless restored some of her equanimity and her ability to think. She remained terribly conscious, though, of the gulf in status between her and this young man Mr. Coventry, and she resolved that she would beg his pardon, as she had been taught to do, and take her leave. To flee immediately made no sense: she could at least gather a few things and take a little while to decide in which direction she should go—even if she kept her resolution not to tell her parents of her flight. She could also, she supposed, endure Mr. Charlton's proposal, in hope that he might turn out to be a better man than Mr. Penny.

All those careful thoughts, however, came crashing down as Mr. Coventry seemed to resolve that he must say what had come into his mind, though some part of his better judgment advised him against the utterance.

"But I know why you were weeping, Miss Eaker. I know you're to be married to George Charlton. And... and you do right to weep, I am sorry to tell you."

Amanda's lips parted, but no sound emerged. Her face glowed and she felt her brow pucker as the tingling of imminent tears began in her nose. Mr. Coventry had on his own face a look of desperate sympathy, and he seemed on the verge of saying something more for a tiny moment that seemed to stretch into an eternity.

Then, he did.

"But I will save you, Miss Eaker. I promise you that I will save you from him."

CHAPTER TWO

George Charlton felt like the Emperor of Durham as he rode to make his proposal to Miss Amanda Eaker.

"Now, Charlton," Lord Rider had said to him the previous day. "Penny got the first of my village maidens, but I think little Amanda's beauty will easily make up for your having to wait. Amanda is a sweet young thing, and I'm told quite bright. She may give you a bit more trouble even than Penny's had with his little Jane, but I think you know how to wield a cane just as well as he does, what?"

The squire chuckled, and George chuckled along with him. "Certainly, my lord," he said. "I don't mind keeping a girl's bottom well marked while she's learning to please a man as she should. My dear departed Louisa, the bride of my youth, felt my punishment strap across her bare backside nearly every day, when we were first married."

Lord Rider, as he often did in such situations, clearly had a good deal of curiosity about the arrangements of George's first marriage. That sort of curiosity, which men like George and his friend Jacob Penny had no hesitation in gratifying, made the squire an excellent companion and friend to men of middle age who enjoyed the seduction and keeping of pretty young women—above all if the seduction and

8

keeping involved strict discipline for the girls.

Lord Rider, it sometimes seemed to George, preferred hearing about the amours and cruelties of others even to engaging in such affairs himself, though the peer did not scruple to whip and to fuck a good many of the girls who came across his path. He awarded more of them, however, to friends like George and Jacob, in hope of hearing stories like the one they had just heard from Jacob, of his first anal love with young Jane, the new Mrs. Penny, who had apparently found the experience quite uncomfortable, if Jacob told it true.

That story, told after dinner over port and cigars, had made for a pleasant masculine evening thus far, and it appeared that George, in payment for the favor of Miss Amanda Eaker's charms, would have the next turn, with a story of disciplining and fucking poor Louisa, dead these six years. Only the dour face of that young friend of Philip Rider's, James Coventry, at Rider Hall to enquire about the prospects of winning the seat in Parliament for the borough of Renford, spoiled the occasion. Lord Rider, however, had enough sense to see that the young man disapproved of the squire's erotic affairs—the seductions of girls of quality in town and the awarding of young brides here at the squire's country seat. Rather than chaffing Coventry on his failure to join in, or asking whether the man had any stories of amorous punishment and pleasure to tell, the master of Rider Hall allowed him to look on disapprovingly, making George wonder whether as the squire enjoyed hearing his friend's stories he also found them piquantly adorned by the disapprobation of the world's more conventional moralists.

"The first Mrs. Charlton didn't come willingly to serve the prick, in the beginning?" Penny asked, clearly reading the squire's desire to hear more just as well as George had, and wishing to facilitate the pleasure of the nobleman who both George Charlton and Jacob Penny regarded as their patron as well as the leader of the little social world of Renford-on-Tees.

George glanced at Coventry, whose face had darkened noticeably, perhaps at the sound of the word *prick*. Penny had told his own story in the allusive manner the men tended to use over the first glass of port, speaking of 'having' and 'enjoying' his young wife's bottom after caning it, rather than of fucking her arse with his stiff prick. With the second glass of port, though, had come the time for coarser discourse, and George had no qualms about telling his story, and discussing the approaching courtship of Miss Amanda Eaker in those terms.

"No, she didn't," George said. "She knew nothing about fucking, of course—only that she had to lie in bed with me, in her shift, and I would tell her what to do. So when I started to raise her shift for the first time, on our wedding night, saying that I wanted to see her cunt and her bubbies because they belonged to me now, she told me I mustn't."

"Oho!" the squire said, delight sparkling in his eyes. "I wager that was a poor decision, where her little bottom was concerned!"

"Yes, my lord," George replied, chuckling. "I got her out of bed, kicking and yelling, and bent her over with her elbows on the counterpane. Louisa probably thought her yells would bring the servants, but she didn't reckon of course on how well servants know what must happen in a bridal chamber."

"I'm sure your butler was listening with his ear at the door," Jacob Penny said with a crooked smile.

"The footmen, too," agreed George. "I held her down over the side of the bed, I pulled up her shift, and I started to spank her nice and hard, to teach her a lesson she wouldn't forget."

"Did you instruct her in her duty, as you punished her?" The words had come from the unexpected quarter of James Coventry, whose face still wore a brooding expression though George thought he could discern that the young man had probably developed a stiff prick despite himself.

"I did, sir. I did," George replied. "I told her that from

then on she would not be permitted to wear even her shift in bed, and I told her that the time had come for fucking. She didn't know the word, of course, but she could tell I didn't mean to be gentle, from the way I kept spanking her. Finally I told her that she need not have any more spanking if she would take off her shift like a good girl, and look at what I had to show her, while I explained what fucking is."

"How red did you get that little bottom, before you stopped?" the squire asked.

"Very red indeed, my lord," George replied, smiling. "I only used my hand that night, but the trouble Louisa had sitting down next day came as much from the spanking as from the fucking I gave her. When she took off the shift, I played with her bubbies and her cunt and bottom for a while, until she realized that my hands could make her feel nice things as well as nasty ones, as long as she proved obedient."

"And then you showed her your manhood?" This question from Coventry made George wonder whether he had misjudged the man: true, he had said *manhood* rather than *prick*, but the tone of the enquiry seemed to indicate that James Coventry did have some experience of such affairs.

"I had her on my knee while I felt her sweet young cunny, until she spent like a little vixen all over my fingers. Then I told her to kneel on the floor, and I lifted my own shirt to show her my cock. 'This,' I said, 'is my prick, darling. It will go inside your cunt, and also your mouth and your bottom, when I choose to put it there. You will get some pleasure, when you have it in your cunt especially, but the purpose of fucking, much as the clergymen will say that it is for getting children, is truly in order that a man may enjoy himself, until his prick spurts out his manly seed where he chooses, whether that be in a girl's cunt, or her mouth, or her anus, or even upon her face, which is pleasant to see sometimes.'"

George delivered this rather embellished account of his

instructions to Louisa on their wedding night in the didactic tone of a priest or a schoolmaster. Both the squire and Jacob Penny responded with applause, and George thought he could see in the candlelight that Coventry's mouth had turned up in a smile.

But the squire loved his fun. "Come now, Charlton. Confess it. In truth you merely said, 'Suck it, little whore,' did you not?"

George chuckled. "In truth, my lord, I did speak to Louisa about fucking, and about my conjugal rights. Perhaps I made her start to suck the prick before I began my discourse though—I will admit that my memory is a little cloudy on that point, since the pleasure of spanking her and fucking her may well have addled my brains a bit."

The squire laughed, and nodded appreciatively. "How did you fuck her the first time?" he asked.

"I stood her up again and told her to bend over the bed just as she had for her spanking."

"You rogue!" Penny said in an approving voice. "You had your bride dog-fashion to deflower her? Did she present like a bitch in heat?"

"I told her to push her bottom out and spread her knees, and she did, though of course she blushed thoroughly at the way she showed me all her most private charms in that posture. Then I put my prick in that tight little cunt and I started to fuck, though I had to hold on tight to her waist to keep her rear end where I wanted it."

"And the servants got their ears' full, I wager," the squire said reflectively.

"They did, my lord."

"As I'm sure they will when you take little Amanda's maidenhead in a fortnight. Though perhaps not even then as much as when you fuck her bottom for the first time, what? As I did with little Jane, I shall have Hoskins tell the parents to ensure their daughter knows she is to furnish every part of her body—mouth, cunt, and anus—to the bridegroom I have chosen."

"Thank you, my lord," George said, bowing his head slightly. He glanced again at Coventry, and found that the brooding expression had resumed its place upon the young man's features.

"Though you'll find, Charlton," Penny said, "that if Miss Amanda Eaker is like her friend Miss Jane Sweetser, stern correction such as it seems you're accustomed to give may well be necessary. I've already told you how much trouble I had getting into Jane's anus, how I had to cane her. It was the same with her mouth, though I promised she would have a new frock if she sucked the prick like a good girl. I had to cane her anyway, though."

"Why don't you make Amanda suck the prick tomorrow, after you propose?" the squire asked with sudden glee. "What a lark, eh?"

George felt a smile break out on his face. He had not thought he would be able to gratify his lust so soon.

"What?" Coventry asked. His face seemed to show warring emotions, as if he couldn't deny that the lewd notion had its appeal even for him, though the moral outrage he felt clearly still predominated. "Send her parents from the parlor and lower his breeches, and command that she suck his prick?"

"Precisely," said the squire. "He'll leave her in no doubt about what's waiting for her on her wedding night. More humane that way, even."

"And if she refuses?"

Penny snorted. "He'll whip her, of course, until she does." He turned to George. "You lucky sod—if only the squire had thought of the idea when I wooed Jane. Fancy raising a girl's petticoats for the strap right after she's accepted you, then spending in her pretty mouth, all in her family's parlor."

The Eaker farm had come into view now, as George rode on with the firm intention of putting these resolutions into effect. He had in his saddlebag the punishment strap he had used upon Louisa's bare backside so many times, and he had an erection so monstrous that riding felt quite uncomfortable.

Yes, Miss Amanda Eaker would accept him, and then she would receive her first libation of her bridegroom's sperm, as she learned from his lips of the sexual duties she must daily perform in his bed, once they were wed in a mere fourteen days' time. If she proved reluctant, she would also learn of how her future husband would punish naughtiness, sobbing out her apology for her disobedience, held down over a chair as the strap fell again and again upon her bare little bottom.

CHAPTER THREE

James Coventry had no time to write to Dr. Brown, but he felt confident he and Miss Eaker would find a welcome at the Scotch physician's unusual institution. He hesitated to involve a girl he had scarcely even met in practices she might find just as troubling as what James had no doubt at all Mr. Charlton would indeed demand of her—*that very day, the bastard,* James thought as he watched the man approach the Eaker farm on horseback along the Durham road. But James' experience with the teaching of Dr. Reginald Brown, late of the Royal College of Surgeons and now the director of his own College of Advanced Study, only a few miles distant in Westmoreland, suggested that although Amanda might make a show of reluctance at first, she would find happiness there.

James had met Dr. Brown in London, on one of the doctor's sojourns in town. Gently expelled from the Royal College but still a member of the Royal Society who found a welcome—if, to be sure, a discreet one—among that body's free-thinking natural philosophers, Dr. Brown spent most of his time in Westmoreland these days, but came up to town at least once a year, during the season, to assist in the dispatch of young ladies in need of relocation.

Not all these young ladies (nor the girls who might scarcely bear the name of *lady*, but who also got the benefit of Dr. Brown's ministrations), James understood, found their way to Dr. Brown's own college. A certain number went to private establishments like those of the Duke of Panton and Sir Gerald Carruthers, while some made an individual journey to the home of one of that class of gentlemen whom Dr. Brown termed 'my proven natural men.'

James Coventry had ambitions in that direction, but he knew he had not yet had a long enough acquaintance with Dr. Brown to request the doctor's aid in bringing Amanda Eaker into James' home straightaway. Too, he felt sure that with further tutelage from the doctor in the training of girls like Amanda he could quite easily become a *proven natural man* himself, but he had self-knowledge enough to see he did not yet deserve that qualification. James had certainly already achieved some little satisfaction in the disciplining and the enjoyment of young women in need of a firm masculine hand, but in Dr. Brown's philosophy he glimpsed the possibility of perfecting those pleasures to a degree that he felt a great zeal to attain. James would gain the doctor's respect and assistance much more readily, he knew, by telling the man honestly that although James recognized in himself a natural man of Dr. Brown's stamp, he understood very well that he did not deserve the honor of having Miss Amanda Eaker delivered directly to him for his pleasure and her training.

Nor could he boast of the wealth necessary to keep her, yet. James had come to Durham and to Rider Hall in hope of coming to an understanding with Lord Rider, of the same kind as those to which he had come with other noblemen and prosperous gentlemen of quality, whereby the younger man would manage the squire's investments in foreign trade. Lord Rider seemed well inclined to James' proposals, as well he might be considering James' skill, experience, and excellent reputation. James thought it quite certain that he could look forward to a future in which he had married his old but financially worthless family name with enough self-made prosperity to keep more than one young lady *under his protection*, one of the phrases employed by Dr. Brown for the special relationships he assisted in establishing.

That future, however, lay at least six months off, and carried perhaps more risk than James liked to contemplate on even his most sanguine days. If he could convince Dr. Brown to enroll Miss Eaker in his college, as the doctor had told James he might do with a girl James brought to his attention, provided James, too, enrolled as the sort of student the doctor called a *cocksman*, he would secure a safe place for Miss Eaker, whatever pecuniary difficulties might befall James himself.

If that place should be a very shameful one, in the eyes of the conventional world whose benighted morality the doctor had taken upon himself to flout, James' complete faith in Dr. Brown's philosophy and methods left no room for doubt that it would in the end tend to her happiness. He would have to share her, of course, with other cocksmen, but he couldn't deny that the thought of watching the girl he had brought enjoyed by other natural men (perhaps several at once) had its own appeal—as did the thought of making Miss Eaker attend his own fucking of other girls. Whether or not he could in the end take Miss Eaker home—perhaps even in the guise of Mrs. James Coventry—his chance encounter with her that morning had convinced him that he must follow the instinct he had conceived the previous evening.

After he had heard the squire's plans for her marriage to Mr. Charlton, and heard Mr. Charlton narrate the despicable, though to be sure very arousing, story of his wedding night with his first wife, James had gone to his bed in Rider Hall in a mild quandary. He wondered even then, though without forming a plan of any kind, whether he should attempt to secure Dr. Brown's assistance in intervening here in Renford-on-Tees. Whoever Miss

Amanda Eaker might be, James thought drowsily, she deserved at least a better husband than this middle-aged lout who had all of a true man's lusts but none of a true man's skill at rendering those lusts' objects happy in their submission to his cock's pleasure.

When he *saw* Miss Amanda Eaker, however, he had instantly fallen into that state that Dr. Brown's teaching had taught him to regard not as *love* (though the doctor made what James considered the soundest possible argument that a true man's desire, tempered with his sympathy and his inborn proclivity toward mercy, constituted what the poets meant by that overused and over-praised sentiment) but as a true man's *attraction* to a girl in need of affectionate mastering. James had suspected he beheld Miss Eaker from the moment he caught sight of the girl sitting in the grove. When he had confirmed that to be her name, he had wondered for a moment, as he beheld her fair, lovely features—her bright blue eyes and her fair hair streaming in disarrangement down her back, as if she had run from her home without thought for it—whether he had the right to work such a transformation in her life and prospects as he contemplated.

Then, as he often did in the presence of feminine beauty, he remembered a passage from Dr. Brown's little book, *On the necessity of men's exercising their masculine rights in erotic matters.*

A natural man never shrinks from his attractions. The young women of our society, raised as they have been within an exhausted morality that seeks to forbid them their natural pleasure in submitting to sexual use by a dominant man, are thereby also rendered fundamentally amenable to such use. When a natural man follows his attraction to a girl, and makes clear to her by the means at his disposal (viz. bare-bottom corporal punishment of various kinds, enforced stimulation of breasts and vulva, anal discipline, etc.) that her body's innate need for erotic submission has a strength her education has attempted to conceal from her, both submissive girl and natural man will achieve the pleasurable aims intended by their Creator.

Before he met Dr. Reginald Brown, James had fucked one girl, a young lady of highly questionable virtue from well before the time he had met her—the questions concerning her ability (or indeed her willingness) to keep her knees closed being of course the reason James had ventured to kiss her in the park of her family's manor. The experience had certainly had a good deal in it that was pleasant, but rutting behind the stable block, the way Miss Portia Harton declared to be her preference, had at once seemed to him too animalistic for his taste and somehow also not truly in line with the essential bestiality of his nature.

That bestiality had troubled him before, as he contemplated his prospects for sating his cock's wayward tendencies, but when he had finally managed to fuck for the first time, there behind the stables, the things that came into his head to do to Miss Harton had caused him to seek the counsel of a physician of whose novel precepts he had previously heard whispers. He had wanted to spank Miss Harton for declining his polite invitation to take his prick in her mouth, for example. He had wanted to bend her over and have her dog-fashion. He had wanted to compel her to receive his manhood in her tiny rear portal, as a much more effective means of contraception than being made to ejaculate upon the grass, and as an erotic act which James instinctually considered would represent a true expression of his mastery.

After Miss Harton declined to suck his cock, however, James had contented himself upon that occasion with the rutting, which he found pleasant enough because he found that he also could at least excite both of them by calling Miss Harton things like *filthy whore* and *sluttish minx*, and telling her quite explicitly of the pleasure he found inside her sweet cunt. He had rutted with Miss Harton three times in the same place, before he had returned to town, and her family had finally managed to marry her off to a Cheapside merchant a month later.

But when James did meet Dr. Reginald Brown, who had come to James' club as the guest of another member—a member James considered a sort of paragon of ethical rakishness, well known for his seductions and the handsome way he treated the girls afterwards—he had been ready with certain questions that had burned themselves into his mind during and after his enjoyment of Miss Harton's illicit favors. He had not at that time had the benefit of reading Dr. Brown's infamous essay, but far from fobbing James off with a suggestion that the young man read the literally seminal work that had given birth to the little movement of which the doctor now served as doyen, the physician had taken an interest in James' obvious confusion.

"How many time did you have coitus with her then, Mr. Coventry?" he had asked when James had outlined his adventure at Harton Manor down in Dorset.

"Three," James replied, proud that he colored only a very little at the doctor's frank language.

"And I venture to say you didn't exercise your natural rights?"

"My natural rights, Dr. Brown? I'm not sure I understand you."

The doctor smiled. "I'm certain you don't, Mr. Coventry. I think I can divine, however, from your interest in speaking with me about your sexual experience and from the generally manly way in which your carry yourself, that you have great promise as what I term a *natural man*. You should certainly read my essay, but I wish also to invite you to choose a girl to enroll in my college in Westmoreland, with yourself as her cocksman."

James couldn't help swallowing hard. He had no idea what the physician meant, at least in any specific way, but he suddenly thought it likely that a course of study at Dr. Brown's college for himself and a girl of his choice could live up to the most lurid of the images that danced across his mental stage. He imagined also that the doctor's curriculum could well prove to resolve James' doubts as to the exercising of his natural rights, whatever precisely they might be, according to Dr. Brown's philosophy.

The clear impropriety of the matter, according to the world's moral conventions, however, still troubled him. "I'm intrigued, Doctor," he said in as measured a tone as he could muster, "but I cannot imagine how I would find such a girl."

Dr. Brown chuckled. "I believe that after you have read my essay, and thought upon it, you will find yourself very quickly in a position where your right, and indeed your duty, to help some unfortunate young woman out of a difficulty by bringing her to me for a thoroughly modern education, will press itself upon you."

Of the things Dr. Brown had said to him, James had credited this one rather less than the Scotsman's more philosophical pronouncements. But the advent of Miss Amanda Eaker into his life came in just such a fashion as the physician had said it would. Right and duty did indeed seem to coalesce in his mind, as he formed his plan to carry her away from Renford-on-Tees and from her monstrous suitor.

CHAPTER FOUR

Amanda had known how difficult it would be to abide in the parlor and listen to the unwelcome protestations of love made to her by Mr. Charlton. She had never imagined, however, how terribly coarse he would make his speech even as he announced his intention to become the happiest man on earth through the bestowal of her hand upon him.

Her parents had simply abandoned her to him at his peremptory request—a request made so churlishly that it more resembled a command—that he be allowed to speak to Miss Eaker privately. Amanda's mother had given her a look that tore the young woman's heart: with her maternal gaze she besought Amanda's pardon while warning her that Mr. Charlton's attentions could not and must not be avoided. All the things to which Mrs. Eaker had alluded in the brief, terrible conversation that followed Amanda's return to the house that morning must befall Amanda, body and soul. She must give her husband his conjugal rights.

But not for a fortnight, her mother said. "You shall have fourteen days to prepare yourself, Amanda. Remember that you will live near us, and that you will have fine things."

"But is he not a bad man, if he wishes to... to make me... *serve* him so?"

Her mother's eyes had told Amanda that Mrs. Eaker did indeed think Mr. Charlton a very bad man, but with her voice she said, "No, child. Husbands... have their conjugal rights. Heaven made women to serve them, as wives, in their houses... and in their beds..."

Mrs. Eaker's voice trailed off, as she seemed to fumble for some way to justify what she had told her daughter of the way she must consent to have her clothing removed, of how she must allow Mr. Charlton to put a thing it seemed he had inside her private places and indeed anywhere else he chose.

"But not for fourteen days," she repeated then, so weakly that Amanda wondered for a moment whether her mother hoped her daughter might avail herself of some private means of escape.

Mrs. Eaker had said that, about the fortnight, Amanda thought as she watched her parents leave the parlor, but the angel... Amanda blushed a little to think of him, of Mr. James Coventry, that way, but how could she do otherwise? She supposed that if his promises proved vain, she might in the end consider him a devil instead, but her hope clung to him now, and she must think him a heavenly messenger of deliverance.

The angel James Coventry had told her that she must expect Mr. Charlton to attempt to take liberties with her today. If he did, she must not worry that Mr. Coventry would abandon her because she had submitted to those shameful liberties. She would, Mr. Coventry feared, have no choice. He himself must make preparations in order to take her away to Westmoreland, but he would return for her in the night, and she must watch for a carriage.

As soon as the parlor door had closed behind her mother, Mr. Charlton, his beady eyes shining with a strange light that seemed to Amanda hungry, and made her heart race with its promise of shame to come, said, "Come here and sit upon my knee, Miss Eaker."

He sat upon the Eakers' best settee, and patted his right

knee. Amanda's eyes widened. Surely he could not expect to *begin* that way? But that beginning led on the instant to conduct so much worse that she almost wished she had obeyed him, and sat upon his green breech-covered knee. She might thereby at least have attempted to discover whether he might be satisfied with a simple acquiescence in that sort of sitting. While for a girl to sit upon a man's knee constituted an accepted part of courtship in many places these days, it still always provoked a blush in the onlooker and an even deeper one in the girl made to assume the position. Perhaps, Amanda thought wildly, if she had consented to it, Mr. Charlton might not have gone on in the terrible way he then did.

"Amanda," the red-faced man said, making her gasp in surprise to be addressed by her Christian name and, even more, in such a brusque way. "I know you've been told you are to be my little wife. I know your mamma has let you know some of the things I'll do to you upon our wedding night and then afterward on our little honeymoon and when you've come to live with me as a wife does with her husband. I'd like to hear you say that you will happily accept my offer of marriage, but that doesn't signify much, as we both know you must consent or your parents will be turned out of their house. So because you won't sit upon my knee, you'll raise your skirts to show me your sweet little cunny, and then you'll kneel and suck my prick until the seed spurts into your belly."

Amanda's jaw hung slack, and her breath came in frightened pants. She half-turned to the parlor door, took a step in that direction, before the odious sound of Mr. Charlton's voice came again to her ears.

"Don't want to give me my rights, girl? Don't want to do your duty?" he said in a sharp, angry tone. "Well, I'll take care of that quick enough!"

She turned to see that he had risen from the settee, and that he had in his right hand a stout, black leather strap about two feet in length.

"You just lay yourself over the settee, miss, and I'll give you your first lesson in a wife's obedience. When I tell you to show me your little cunt, from now on, you'll do it, and the same with sucking my prick, because you'll remember that your husband knows how to discipline a young bride. I did it with my Louisa, and I'll do it with you. If you want to sit comfortably at your own table, girl, you'll give me my conjugal rights like a good 'un."

Amanda froze solid as a block of ice at these words, and at the advancing tread of Mr. Charlton's feet in their muddy riding boots. He stood only a foot from her, his angry red face seeming to scorch her own with the heat of her blush at the terrible things he said.

"What will it be, girl?" he asked, with scorn in his voice now that Amanda assumed must represent mockery of her pretensions of having any choice in the matter. "Will you get over the settee and have your whipping like a good girl, or will I have to put you there and hold you down while I give it to you?"

She didn't think she could ever have obeyed him, so it was almost a mercy when he took firm hold of her upper arm and drew her past him and toward the dear little settee with the embroidered cushion of which Mrs. Eaker was so fond. Amanda's mind occupied itself with a dilemma that even in her panic she knew meant nothing of importance: should she scream, in some hope that her parents might put a stop to this, at least for today?

But as the man who claimed a wish to be her loving bridegroom pushed her to her knees and roughly forced her face down into the settee's embroidery of pink and red flowers, she knew that her parents would not come, could not come to her aid. If Amanda cried out, they would merely have to listen to their daughter's first thrashing by her bridegroom.

She felt Mr. Charlton's hands lifting her skirts, and could not help crying out at the terribly undignified sensation of the air moving inside her drawers. Amanda, shaped as she was by her education in Mrs. Bates' schoolroom and at her mother's knee knew well that a young lady, even the daughter of a working farmer like Miss Amanda Eaker, never allowed her skirts to be raised that way.

"Oho!" exclaimed Mr. Charlton. "What pretty drawers you have, Miss Amanda Eaker, with a fine lace border, such as a lady of quality might wear!"

Amanda had thought her face could not get hotter, but now she felt herself blush to the roots of her hair. It seemed inconceivable that any man—let alone a man like Mr. Charlton—should lay eyes on her pretty drawers, a present from her aunt who had gone to Paris the previous spring, but now he had not just seen them, but…

"We must have them down, though, must we not?" Mr. Charlton said, and then Amanda felt him undo the ribbon that cinched the waist.

"Oh, please," she cried. "Please don't, Mr. Charlton. I'll…"

"Don't talk nonsense, girl," the man said gruffly. "You shan't escape your whipping now."

She felt the strap in his right hand brush along her flank as he drew down her drawers, and the two impressions together forced a little sob from her throat. She made a wild resolution not to make another sound, in hope of sparing her parents the shame and anguish of hearing the way her bridegroom used their sweet young daughter.

"I can look at your cunt perfectly well this way, though, I suppose," came his mocking voice, thin and reedy but entirely capable of striking fear and shame into Amanda's heart. "Spread these knees a bit, and I'll have a look between your thighs, and your bum-cheeks too."

Her resolution flew away, and she sobbed again as he enforced his crude desire, pulling her knees apart as far as the loose drawers that now lay about her knees would allow.

"That's a sweet little puss," said Mr. Charlton. "Neater and smaller than my Louisa's, too, and tighter for my fucking, I'm sure. What pretty blond curls you have,

Amanda Eaker. Let's see how whorish a nature you have, now."

Having no idea what he could mean, Amanda twisted her head around to try to see what Mr. Charlton would do.

"Put that pretty face in the cushion, girl," he said angrily. "I'm having some of my conjugal rights, now, and you must keep your face respectfully lowered. Soon enough I'll fuck you this way, dog-fashion as we men call it, in your cunt and then your bottom, and you will learn to bite your pillow, as my Louisa did, to endure my pleasures. A sound whipping today will be a fine preparation."

Then, without warning, he touched her where she knew she must not even touch herself: where only a wedded husband may touch. Amanda shuddered, trembled, and then to her horror realized that Mr. Charlton's hand felt *pleasant*, though in a strange and terrible way.

"Oh, no," she whispered. The heat was in her face again, but it was also down there, and she felt wetness, too.

"You *are* a little whore, Amanda Eaker," Mr. Charlton said in a voice that sounded much more satisfied than any he had used previously. "When it's time to put my cock in this virgin cunny, I'll slip the head right into your sweet slit, before I ride hard and take your maidenhead. You'll get it like this, bent over with your face down, dog-fashion, so I can play with this little bottom while I fuck."

Amanda moaned, her senses and her thoughts all in a whirl, so confused she thought she might never be able to reason again. How could her body seem to cry out for what the odious Mr. Charlton did to it? What he said he would do, soon, though Amanda scarcely understood what he meant by his sharp-sounding coarseness, *pricks* and *cocks* and *fucking*.

When he spoke of her bottom, his touch left her cunny, and with both his hands he spread her open there. "A prim little arsehole, too," he said. "An even tighter ride for a husband who knows what he's about."

Amanda sobbed again, as her bottom tried to clench, to

close against him. Mr. Charlton held it open, though, and she gave a little cry as he put his forefinger upon the tiny flower and pushed gently.

"I'll break you in slowly, here, little filly, if you're a good girl," he said. "A perfect anus like this one needs tenderness before it's ready for fucking."

The hands left her; the cheeks of her bottom closed. Amanda bit her lower lip as she looked at the pink embroidered flowers. She would *try* not to cry out.

"Put those knees together, girl," Mr. Charlton said, his voice angry once again. "You must have your whipping now, and you must not get the wrong idea about your cunt. I'll bring out your whorishness as I like and when I like, but when the time for discipline has come, there will never be any pleasure for you. How could you learn your lesson otherwise?"

CHAPTER FIVE

Dr. Reginald Brown read Mr. Coventry's note with interest.

My dear Dr. Brown,

I must write in haste, and come to the point immediately. I hope you will not scruple to receive me and a Miss Amanda Eaker at your college. Miss Eaker will otherwise either be subject to a monstrous marriage with a man forty years her senior or be forced to flee her home and, I fear, ultimately to come upon the town. As there is no alternative, I shall not wait for your reply but shall instead remove Miss Eaker with me, to your house, this very night. If you turn us away, I must, I suppose, then journey further with her and hope to keep her in town until I can put my pecuniary affairs in enough order so as to permit my marrying her and attempting to train her in the ways of a natural union myself, though the risks of my position make me less than sanguine that I shall be able to keep Miss Eaker for long, and I fear she may in despair fall prey to the blandishments of the procuress and the panderer. I do venture to hope that you will be as good as your word, however, and enroll Miss Eaker as a submissive maiden and myself as a cocksman under your roof. Though I imagine that according to your philosophy it will not much signify, my own remaining scruples at carrying off Miss Eaker are put to rest by the way her odious suitor

29

has already taken terrible liberties with her person, viz. to whip her, to fondle her private places, and to deprive the poor girl of the virginity of her mouth, if I may use such a phrase.

I must away to hire the carriage, but I am, sir, in hope that this entreaty will not fall upon deaf ears, coming as it does from

Your obedient servant and, heaven willing, cocksman,

James Coventry

Dr. Brown rang for Andrews, the good and faithful servant who served at once as his butler and as the chief porter of the College of Advanced Study.

"Andrews," the doctor said when the man, at fifty-two just a few years older than Brown himself, appeared, "we shall have an arrival before dawn."

"A girl alone, sir?"

"No, a girl and a cocksman, Mr. Coventry. The girl may have the cell at the end of the third floor corridor. The cocksman may rest in the meadow room tonight and tomorrow. We shall move him into the dormitory tomorrow evening, though of course he will spend the night in his young lady's cell. He will room in with Mr. Stallings, with whom I believe he is already acquainted."

"Very good, sir," Andrews said, and vanished to make the necessary preparations.

Dr. Brown took a crisp new piece of paper from his drawer, and began to write.

Mr. James Coventry, cocksman, and Miss Amanda Eaker, young lady

He checked in a little leather-bound book that sat at the edge of his desk.

Case 35
April, 1875
Cocksman presents as a natural man in the middle stages of freeing himself from the shackles of his conventionally moralistic education.

Has reported coitus with a girl in a conventional fashion, leading (as often with such young men) to thoughts of the sexual mastery more appropriate to his character.

Young lady is apparently escaping an ill-sorted marriage, though it appears the would-be bridegroom has somewhat initiated her, and the girl may be rather farther along than most virgins, at enrollment.

Initial plan of treatment: 1) thorough medical examination of young lady, with cocksman present to discuss course of study; 2) period of study and adjustment; 3) defloration of young lady by cocksman; 4) advanced sexual training with multiple cocksmen and observation of other couples having coitus.

Dr. Brown filed the paper away, smiling broadly. What a splendid addition Mr. Coventry and his young lady would be to the college! And the girl to arrive already with so many questions about what her monstrous suitor had demanded of her!

He rose from his desk and began his evening rounds.

Three couples were in residence at the College of Advanced Study, and a further two young women were undergoing training for natural men who had commissioned Dr. Brown and his staff to prepare the girls for keeping when they had completed their studies with the doctor. Of the couples, Mr. Shaw and Miss Reynolds had advanced the furthest in their treatment: they would soon leave Westmoreland for America, where other disciples of Dr. Brown had established communities in which men might exercise their natural rights in ways still impossible in England.

Not every cocksman who studied at Dr. Brown's college elected to take his girl so far away; the wealthier among them could afford to conceal from censorious eyes their natural enjoyment of young women trained for their pleasure, or indeed simply to bear the brickbats hurled by those of hypocritical, upstanding morality. Such prosperous men as Dr. Brown supposed James Coventry would soon become, if the doctor had heard the truth of it, could run a household along natural lines, the wife or mistress for example frequently naked in the drawing room in front of the servants, and merely be called *eccentric*.

The doctor went first to Miss Reynolds' cell, a cozy one on the third floor, to which she had graduated after Mr. Shaw deflowered her. He opened the door without knocking and stepped into the room to find Mr. Shaw enthusiastically enjoying his girl's bottom atop the large bed. Stella Reynolds was on all fours, entirely naked, and she cried out with every thrust of Joseph Shaw's stiff penis into her still-tight anus.

Dr. Brown could see the anal coitus clearly because Mr. Shaw had taken the spread-legged crouching position the doctor recommended for this mode of natural enjoyment. Miss Reynolds' lovely pink labia, shaved of their curls of course just as Miss Eaker's soon would be, were fully visible to Dr. Brown's assessing eye just below the place where her natural man drove his erection in over and over. He also observed, and noted in his rounds book, that Miss Reynolds bore the distinctive marks of the birch rod upon her buttocks.

"I'm very sorry to interrupt you, Mr. Shaw," the doctor said. "I won't be a moment, though." He moved around the bed so that he could speak to the lovers face to face.

Miss Reynolds gave a little shriek of shame at the sound of the doctor's voice and the sight of his presence at her anal session. Dr. Brown noted that, too: he would consult with Mr. Shaw to find ways, as he and Miss Reynolds continued their natural union, to lessen and even someday eliminate her shame. Perhaps public coitus in their new American home might suit: Miss Stella Reynolds displayed naked in the town square, then enjoyed by her husband over a bench, in the view of passersby. On the American frontier, it seemed one could create a community where such things might occur, and thus the possibilities for ridding the world of erotic hypocrisy seemed to Dr. Brown virtually limitless.

Mr. Shaw had slowed his thrusting in Miss Reynolds'

anus, but as an advanced student he knew that when Dr. Brown made his rounds he liked to have his students continue whatever sexual activity he found them engaged in, while he made his daily observations. He therefore continued to pump his penis in and out of his girl's fundament, as Brown began to ask his few brief questions.

"That's very fine anal coitus, Mr. Shaw. Very fine. I see Miss Reynolds has been birched. Why was that?"

"Miss Reynolds was reluctant to present her bottom, Doctor."

Mr. Shaw spoke in a voice that betrayed only a little strain. His hands continued to grip Miss Reynolds' hips firmly, as Dr. Brown always recommended. Miss Reynolds, for her part, had closed her eyes as if to lessen her shame at having the physician witness what she still considered the ordeal of her sexual use by her protector. Dr. Brown made a note, though, that her brow had creased in obvious arousal, and that she bit her lip to keep from voicing the lascivious feelings Mr. Shaw's hard penis awoke in her.

Dr. Brown clucked with his tongue. "We've discussed this, have we not, Miss Reynolds?"

The sweet dark-haired girl's brown eyes flew open and she looked at Dr. Brown with a dazed expression. Mr. Shaw drove his cock into her narrow rear passage again, and she gave a little whimper.

"How you are to be ready to present any part of your body, with no false modesty, to the natural man who cares for you and who has taken responsibility for you?"

"Yes, Doctor," she moaned, as Mr. Shaw slowly made his outward stroke.

Dr. Brown turned back to the cocksman. "Next time, Mr. Shaw, I might try the lap technique we discussed, rather than the birch or the strap. Most accomplished natural men find it's best to ensure some variety, if you take my meaning?"

Mr. Shaw nodded. The *lap technique* involved sitting a clothed girl on the cocksman's lap and fondling her under her petticoats until she begged to *present* her charms for his enjoyment, as Dr. Brown named the essential gestures he taught young women like Miss Reynolds to make, one for each of the three natural paths of masculine pleasure: mouth, vulva, and anus.

"Yes, Doctor," said Mr. Shaw.

"Carry on, then," Dr. Brown said, closing his book with a smile. As he made his way back into the corridor and closed the door behind him, the increasingly rapid rhythm of the bedsprings made him smile.

Miss Booth and Miss Dixon were having a modesty lesson with Sister Stone, in the tiled training room that boasted a drain in its center toward which the floor sloped. Dr. Brown entered just as the two young ladies, both of good family but just now both completely naked and red-faced, were peeing on themselves, at Sister Stone's command. Forbidden even to squat, let alone use the pot, they watched their golden urine trickle, then rush down their thighs, both whimpering a little at the feeling.

"There, girls," said the wise, middle-aged Sister Stone, dressed in the severe frock of a nurse. "That feels better, doesn't it?"

"Yes, sister," said little blond Deborah Booth, whose inner labia peeped saucily out from the tidily depilated cleft between her now liberally bedewed thighs.

"Yes, sister," said willowy, auburn-haired Thea Dixon, whose vulva presented much more modestly.

"How are these young ladies today, sister?" Dr. Brown asked.

Sister Stone said in her broad Yorkshire tones, "Miss Dixon has been a good girl, but you must ask Miss Booth whether she intends to change her bashful ways."

He turned to the adorable blond girl. "What happened, Miss Booth?" he asked.

Miss Booth looked down at her urine-soaked feet and the trickle of both girls' pee making its way across the white tiles to the drain.

"I had to take her over my knee for a spanking, is what happened, Doctor," said the sister. "She wouldn't play with herself when I told her to."

Dr. Brown looked intently at Miss Booth. "Look at me, Deborah," he said, and she turned her blue eyes to his and widened them. "You must do as sister says, do you understand?"

"But I did it, after she spanked me!" The pert little nose twitched, but not, he thought, in defiance; rather in hope that she could somehow have exceptions made for her. Girls frequently took a long while to understand that such exceptions would render their training almost meaningless: training a girl for a natural man's pleasure involved awakening in her the need for complete, shameless sexual obedience.

"You must learn to masturbate without being spanked, Deborah," he said patiently. "Now, when your master Mr. Graham had coitus with you for the first time, I believe that he spanked you first. Is that right?"

"Yes, Doctor," said Miss Booth, frowning a little as if trying to follow his train of thought.

"And so, though perhaps you did not even know it yourself, you needed to be spanked before you would touch your vulva. You must learn to do that, and whatever else he commands, when Mr. Graham requires it of you, whether or not he punishes you first."

He turned from Miss Booth's still-puzzled face to Sister Stone. "Sister, after they've cleaned each other up, please work them on the double masturbation saddle for fifteen minutes, facing one another. Watching Miss Dixon climax while she does the same may help Miss Booth let go of her reliance on punishment."

He went finally to the door of the grand bedroom, as he had named the large salon-like space that held three large beds as well as several divans and punishment horses. He looked in at the peephole designed for his observation, and saw as he expected that Mr. Stallings and Mr. Hudson had exchanged girls for an exercise in side-by-side coitus: on the central bed Mr. Stallings had coitus with Miss Miller on the left and Mr. Hudson with Miss Parker on the right.

The couples both copulated in the side-lying position, but Mr. Stallings had laid Miss Miller on her left side, while Mr. Hudson had put Miss Parker on her right, so that the girls must face one another and each must watch her own master enjoy another girl, while of course feeling her own vagina enjoyed by another cocksman. Dr. Brown did not go in, but merely observed the expressions upon the girls' faces: side-by-side coitus first with a natural man's own girl and then later with another man's, loaned for the occasion, constituted a very important part of the curriculum at the College for Advanced Study, one so intense that Dr. Brown never interrupted it.

On the faces of Beatrix Miller and Cressida Parker, he saw the submission for which he looked: their understanding of how much pleasure they gave Mr. Hudson and Mr. Stallings by simply letting their natural men watch them as they themselves watched the shameful spectacle of hard penises in tight vaginas—the penis that belonged in each girl's own vagina thrusting into the other girl's instead. With it he saw the arousal this submission gave, layered atop the animal arousal of the coitus itself. The girls cried out as their masters swung their hips to drive their erections so deep inside that the girls' young buttocks came up against the sinewy laps of the men.

Miss Amanda Eaker would cry out the same way in a few weeks' time, Dr. Brown thought with a smile, whether in subjection to the hard penis of her protector and master, Mr. Coventry, or to another cocksman's. Side-by-side coitus would become as much a part of her life as it had become for Miss Miller and Miss Parker—and for every young woman of Dr. Brown's college.

CHAPTER SIX

At midnight, when all was quiet, James had the carriage wait five hundred yards down the road from the Eaker farm so that the noise of the horses would not wake Miss Eaker's parents or their one servant, a maid-of-all-work. From behind the barn, Miss Eaker came to him, walking very stiffly. Her eyes, in the dim light of a waning moon, looked red and puffy.

James took her hands and gazed into her face, anger at Charlton rising in his breast, but knowing they must hurry and not wanting to bring back to Miss Eaker's mind what he felt sure she had undergone at the monster's hands.

"He…" she started. "He…"

"Hush now, darling," James said, the endearment seeming to come so naturally to him that he scarcely noticed himself uttering it. "We can talk in the carriage."

He put his arm around her waist, and to his elation she clung to him as they walked to where the coachman waited impassively. When they had nearly reached the door that the man held open, he doffed his cap with his other hand and said, "Is that you, Miss Eaker?"

She drew back a little, but then she spoke in a choked voice. "Yes, Mr. Podgins. I… I… am going away."

The coachman gave her a gentle smile that James could just make out in the moonlight. "That's all right, miss," he said. "I won't tell a soul as it was I who helped you elope with your fine gentleman. I don't doubt as you're right to do it, with what they're saying in the village."

James had a momentary pang of guilt that the elopement in question would not be of the sort Podgins probably imagined, but he still had no doubt that he had lit upon the only solution available to Amanda Eaker's difficulty.

"Thank you, Mr. Podgins," she said. "Perhaps... perhaps you might tell my parents?"

Podgins nodded. "I shall, if you wish it, Miss Eaker." He looked at James.

"That's all right," James said shortly. "Quite all right." He handed the coachman a shilling. Podgins replaced his hat on his head to take it.

"Thank you, sir," he said. "Thank you very kindly."

"There's a half-crown at the other end if we reach the house in Westmoreland by daybreak. You're not to tell Miss Eaker's people our destination, mind. You may say that she will write when she is settled."

"Westmoreland?" Amanda asked, in some confusion. "I had thought... that is to say... are you not from Dorset, Mr. Coventry? Shall we take the railroad, then?"

Podgins gave James a look that seemed to say that the coachman would have no mental difficulty in bringing James and Amanda to the gates of Hades, if she went thither to escape Mr. George Charlton, and a half-crown awaited him from the man who had hired him. Young ladies who eloped even in 1875 could not expect to have any more say in where their lovers took them than their counterparts of the libertine eighteenth century had enjoyed: if James wished to take the girl straight to a London brothel, there to keep her as a whore, Podgins would have sighed a bit over it, perhaps, but gladly spent the fee he got from it. Westmoreland probably seemed to him a highly respectable place by comparison.

"Please get into the carriage, Miss Eaker," James said. "I shall explain once we are on our way."

He urged her forward, and though her steps to the coach door were slower and more reluctant than they had been from the barn, she went, and they were soon ensconced upon the seat, side by side, and Podgins had closed the door, stepped up onto the box, and quietly got the horses walking.

"Why do we go so slowly?" Amanda asked.

"We must pass through the village as quietly as we can," James explained patiently. "With any luck, no one will know that you have gone until we are at the college."

"The college?" A frown appeared on her face. "Are you a... a teacher, then?"

"No, darling," James replied. He took her hands in his. "Try to listen carefully to what I will tell you now."

Amanda's eyes widened, as if she had heard something in his voice that frightened her. It did not surprise James, since from Dr. Brown's essay that he must now set his hand to the plow of training her. No soft words would do, now: in the eyes of the world—which meant, at the moment, Amanda Eaker's eyes as well—his plans for her defloration and sexual training at the College of Advanced Study would appear monstrous. If he did not own that seeming monstrosity, he had learned from the physician's writing, he could not in time demonstrate how natural Amanda's sexual service to him would soon be.

The first suggestion to a young woman that a man's natural erotic rights supervene the false and pernicious modesty and shame thrust upon her by her so-called education in conventional morality will always be greeted with indignation, Brown wrote. *One important test of a man's ability to foster in himself his own manly nature, difficult as it is in this benighted day and age, will be seen in whether he can resolve to teach the young woman he chooses to train for his sexual pleasure the first important lesson: that nature has fashioned her to obey him, and him to enjoy her obedience. Not one man in ten, in my judgment, has it in him today to make himself a truly natural man. Not one in ten can look a blushing young woman in the eye and tell her that from henceforth she will learn to yield up to him the secret places of her body and her most intimate charms, in order that he may use them for his pleasure. Today's natural man must become his true self not as men did in ages past, when a young man grew up in the knowledge that he might enjoy himself erotically with the girl of his choice, provided she did not belong to another man of his class, but, as I see it, lifting himself up as it were by his own bootstraps.*

"I have saved you from Mr. Charlton," James began.

A little smile broke out on Amanda's face at that, and her sweet, pale lips parted as if to express her thanks, but James continued, making clear to her that when he spoke, she must listen and wait her turn.

"But I must now tell you that your salvation will be very different from what you expect."

Amanda's eyes went wide again at that—much wider than they had when he had a moment ago instructed her to listen to him.

"Do you mean to say that you will not... not m-marry me?"

Of course that would be her conventional, worldly concern, would it not. A tear appeared in the corner of her eye. For a moment—no longer than the blink of an eye—James wondered if he did have it in him to make himself a natural man *lifting himself up by his own bootstraps.*

Then, however, he knew that he could, and the words and arguments—sound reasoning though he knew Amanda would take some while to see it thus—came to him as if by inspiration.

"I may well marry you, Miss Eaker," James said, making his voice gentle now. She frowned, as if confused by the hypothetical way in which he had spoken. "But a connection of marriage is not why I have brought you away from your home, and rescued you from that odious man who would never have allowed you a day's joy in your life after you had married him."

A tear appeared in Amanda's eye, rolled down her cheek. James put out his fingertip to touch it, and Amanda shivered. Suddenly he held her face in both his hands and kissed her as he had longed to kiss for so long. Amanda yielded up her mouth to his and her body to his embracing arms, and a sighing whimper of pleasure she could perhaps not even have described came from her chest as he kissed and kissed again.

When James broke the fifth or sixth kiss, he held her in silence for a while, as she panted, nearly breathless, within the circle of his arms.

"Tell me what he did to you," he said softly. Then, again, the inspiration—the power to lift himself by his bootstraps—came to him from within, and he spoke further. He said, in an even, low voice intended to convince Amanda both of how seriously he took the matter and of how well he understood why she had whimpered when he kissed her, even if she did not. "Whatever it was, though, it is of the utmost importance that you understand that everything he did, or made you do, is undoubtedly something that I will also require of you."

Amanda shuddered in his arms, and the shudder seemed for a moment almost to become a struggle to free herself from James' embrace.

From the box, suddenly, Podgins called, "Ha!" and the reins jingled. The horses hastened to a trot, and then a very fast canter. The carriage began to sway, and the wind to whistle by the slightly open windows.

Again Amanda moved, tried to twist, but again James held her fast, not roughly but very firmly. "Tell me," he commanded.

She gave a little sob into the shoulder of his coat. "He whipped me," she said. "He whipped me so hard."

If Amanda had felt nothing ambiguous about Charlton's misbegotten attempt at premarital discipline, James knew her voice would have sounded very different. He knew instinctually that the vicissitudes of her situation—the

41

knowledge of what had happened to her friend Jane at the mercy of Mr. Penny, the idea that she would undergo similar dreadful trials, and perhaps above all her expectation of being carried away from it all by James himself—had made the experience of the whipping a morbidly erotic one. Her self-proclaimed bridegroom's punishment strap, falling again and again upon her bare bottom in order to teach Amanda obedience to his erotic whims, had to her great confusion awakened in her just the feelings that a natural man must enlist to make her happy—and him along with her.

So James took the way his cock had hardened at her words as the sign of his incipient mastery, and he said, "And then?"

She gave another sob. "Then... I-I h-had to kneel in front of him..." Her voice trailed off.

"He made you suck his cock," James said, knowing that to help her thus would move her submission further along.

She nodded against his shoulder. "H-he called it his... his prick, but..."

"Yes," James said. "That part of a man has a great many names. Did he spend in your mouth? Did he make you swallow his seed?"

Amanda nodded again. "It was..." Again James heard in her voice the ambiguity that showed that new feelings had begun to unfold in her breast—and, he felt sure, new sensations had started to take hold between her thighs. He imagined, too, that her whipped bottom must be aiding in those sensations' stirring. "I didn't like it."

"Darling, if I told you that you must suck *my* cock, and swallow my seed, do you think that you would like it better?"

"Oh," Amanda said very softly. Her body stiffened for a moment, though without a renewal of the delicious squirming, and then seemed to give up its tension and to relax in his arms, a feeling even more delightful than the squirming had been. James moved his hands to hold the back of her head, gently, and to twine his fingers in her soft hair. He turned her face to his and kissed her, much more softly than he had at first, his tongue less demanding now but still seeking to teach his girl that she must receive what it pleased him to give.

"Oh," she said again, when he had broken the kiss. "Must I do it now?"

"No, not yet," he said, his cock however growing even stiffer at the submission in her voice, "but soon. This is what I must tell you. I am taking you to a place where you will learn to give me my own conjugal rights, and to please me with your young body's charms, but not as you would have done for that oaf who whipped you and made you suck today. Whether or not we become man and wife, darling, I will undertake to make you the happiest girl in the world, even as you yield up to me all your modesty, and cry out under my mastery."

"But…" Amanda pleaded. "But… you cannot. I m-must… Mr. Podgins!"

In her face, James saw a resistance that he knew must come from the propriety of her upbringing, and he knew immediately what he must do.

"Hush, darling," he said. "Mr. Podgins will not stop for you, but only for me. And now I must punish you for attempting it. Lay yourself over my lap."

Amanda hesitated, but James knew he must show her the strength of his resolution, in order to ensure she felt secure in his protection. Though she struggled, he pulled her down over his thighs and raised her skirts, nothing loath to see the lovely bottom he knew would now belong to him, or to spank her—if gently, seeing the treatment Charlton had given her—to teach her that he intended to exercise his right in that regard as well.

She whimpered as he pulled down her drawers, and he did indeed have a pang of guilt when he saw the tracery of red and purple left by Charlton's wicked strap. Amanda Eaker's bottom looked so lovely in the moonlight that

James could not resist caressing it before he chastised her, but when he heard her whimpers change to moans of pleasure he knew he must proceed to the punishment, and he did. He raised his hand and brought it down firmly, over and over.

"Will you call out to stop the carriage again?" he asked after he had spanked her ten times.

Amanda sobbed, her bottom squirming under his hand, and she writhed under his left arm as he held her fast. The marks from Charlton's strap had grown livid, and James knew that whether or not she capitulated he must stop the punishment soon—though the sight fired his blood so extremely that he also knew he would have trouble restraining himself from taking further liberties despite knowing Dr. Brown would wish him to wait.

But to his great happiness, Amanda whispered, "No, sir. I am sorry."

James contented himself with a final caress of her round little bottom, and then he restored her drawers and her skirts, and took her back into his arms. Amanda cried out her grief and her distress into his shoulder, then fell asleep a few moments after a whispered "Thank you, Mr. Coventry" that brought joy to James' heart.

CHAPTER SEVEN

The barest hint of grey light had begun in the East, behind the carriage, when they arrived at the big manor house. Amanda had fallen asleep in the swaying carriage an hour before, with James' arm around her, after he had gently said, to her alarmed questions, that the ways of the house—the college—to which he now brought her required that she know no more than the terrible things he had told her so far: terrible, and yet somehow each one with some strange, ready analogue already inside her soul.

As she woke with the carriage's stopping at last, and looked out in her first awareness of the Tudor manor house that loomed out the coach window, those terrible things came back into her mind, broken out from her angel's address to her into separate propositions, or perhaps—Amanda thought with something between a shudder and a shiver—promises.

You will learn to please me.
You will yield up your modesty.
You will cry out under my mastery.
You will suck my cock.
You will be the happiest girl in the world.

Married girls were always the happiest girls in the world,

weren't they? And James, her angel, said that he *might well* marry her. *What a funny thing to say*, Amanda thought, in the dispassionate way that a person may think, upon waking, even of an idea so very material to their well-being and contentment as her marriage.

Her angel had said it, too, in a way that suggested that he meant more by it simply than that he had not yet decided whether Amanda were worth wedding, or even that she would now stand her trial, here at this mysterious institution. James had said that he *might* marry Amanda as if marrying her did not matter to him—*no, rather, as if I must not regard marriage as that which will make me the happiest girl in the world.*

Dear Mr. Podgins opened the coach door, and James alit, handing the coachman the promised half-crown. As he turned to hand Amanda out of the carriage, she saw a man who must be the butler of the house (surely colleges didn't have butlers?) emerge from the grand front door.

If marriage would not make her happy, what would? Mrs. Bates, and Amanda's mother, had—she suddenly realized—given her this single standard of happiness, had they not? That a girl married, and lived happily with her husband.

Jane had married, and Jane had found herself strapped down to a trestle and caned by Mr. Penny, until at her husband's command she begged for his prick up her bottom, and he gave it to her long and hard. Amanda had been going to be married to Mr. Charlton, and she had found herself whipped in her own family's parlor, then sucking her so-called bridegroom's stiff manhood until he spurted his burning, bitter seed down her throat.

To marry, in the storybooks, meant to keep house and care for children, and perhaps some girls experienced that sort of union with good, industrious husbands. Amanda supposed that when she first saw James Coventry she had thought that perhaps he would make that sort of husband, and when he said he would save her, that idea had grown in strength.

But at the very same time another notion as to what sort of man her angel might be had traveled by the side of the first, one that had a dark attraction for her. Might James not also be the sort of man who would… *guide* her? She blushed even to think of it in those terms, but in the carriage he had given her other terms, too—much more shameful ones.

For it seemed he was indeed the sort of man to guide her: in pleasing him, in yielding to him, in obeying him even when he told her to take his hardness in her mouth, between her legs, up her bottom.

Was it not even worse then, that a man should tell a girl he would *guide* her that way and, well, *use* her that way, without a promise of marriage, than that a recognized suitor or a wedded husband should demand such shameful service? As Amanda took her angel's hand and stepped from the carriage, looking around her at the grandeur of the isolated park surrounding the enormous house whose farther reaches remained shrouded in darkness, she couldn't answer the question. She felt sure Mrs. Bates would say that it was much, much worse—that it would have been far better to have stayed in Renford-on-Tees and to have submitted to the pleasures of Mr. Charlton, the whippings and the other thing he had said… Amanda whispered it even in her mind: *fucking*.

"Mr. Coventry, is it?" the butler asked.

"It is," James said, "and Miss Eaker." He led Amanda forward a little.

"I am Mr. Andrews, porter of the college."

Porter, Amanda thought. *That's what colleges have.*

"I've only the one valise," James said, as Podgins handed it down from the carriage.

"A junior porter will see to that," Andrews said. "The young lady has no baggage, I imagine."

Amanda studied Andrews' face. The blood had rushed to her face at this reminder of her shameful status: a young woman, a *miss*, traveling alone with a gentleman. Had the porter's voice implied that she didn't deserve to receive any of the customary respect accorded a *miss*, because she had clearly come to his house for immodest reasons?

If his voice did imply it, his face remained impassive as it looked into James', and Amanda had no way to determine whether that expression indicated delicacy or distaste.

"No, that's right," James said. He turned to the coachman. "Thank you, Mr. Podgins," he said warmly. "Have a good journey back to Renford."

Mr. Podgins tipped his cap, and gave Amanda a little smile. "Best of luck, miss," he said. "I shall tell your parents you'll write, and I'm sure it will be with happy news."

"Thank you, Mr. Podgins," Amanda replied, thinking that once the man had departed, she would be entirely in the power of James Coventry and his friends at this 'college,' whoever they might be. She shivered despite the relative warmth of the air on this spring morning.

Podgins got up, and turned the carriage around the broad circle of the drive before the house. He tipped his cap a final time, and then the horses took him quickly out of sight along the Durham road.

She turned back to Andrews, expecting to be told where the master or mistress of the house—or perhaps the don? or tutor?—would receive them. Instead, the man said to James, "The young lady will have to take off her clothes now. The head sister will come and fetch her in a moment, and bring her to her cell. Dr. Brown has just risen, and will meet you in the breakfast room for a brief word, and after that I will show you to your bedroom."

For a long moment, Amanda truly did believe that her roiling fancies had deceived her ears, and that Andrews had actually said something more like *The young lady will have need of refreshment*. But James turned to her with an expression that mingled apology with something else—something that alarmed her even as it made her feel that same yielding that had seemed to possess her when he kissed her in the carriage.

"You must take off everything, darling," he said. "Gown, petticoats, corset—"

Trying desperately to find some small thing on which to pin a hope, she said, "Surely not my shift or my drawers?"

James glanced at Andrews, whose face remained impassive. Then turned his gaze back to Amanda, his brow now more set, his eyes narrower. The alarm rose inside her, but so did the fluttery, yielding feeling that quickened her breath even more, it seemed, than the fear did.

"Those too, darling. You must be naked when you enter the college."

"But—"

"This instant, Amanda."

"But I have no one to help me undress!" Her mother always helped her, and she her mother, so as not to tax the already overtaxed maid-of-all-work.

But just then a woman, wearing the garb of a nursing sister—black frock and white apron, with the snow-white cap atop her grey curls—emerged from the door.

"Does the young lady require assistance?" the woman said in a voice whose supercilious authority belied the words' solicitude. She stepped toward Amanda, and Amanda instinctually shied away, trying to remove her hand from James'.

He held her fast though, with a disapproving look upon his face. "Yes, sister," he said. "Miss Eaker would be grateful for your help in undressing. Wouldn't you, darling?"

Amanda felt her face pucker toward tears as she looked from James' handsome, unyielding face to the nursing sister's much less attractive though equally unyielding one. "I don't understand," she whispered. "Why... why must I undress... outdoors?"

The sister turned to James. "Mr. Coventry, my name is Sister Stone. I shall take care of this little trouble, with my strap if necessary. You should go in and talk to Dr. Brown, and then get your rest. When Miss Eaker is ready for her examination, I shall let the doctor know, and he will rouse you for it. You'll see Miss Eaker's charms then, I promise."

"Very well," James said, but he did not drop Amanda's hand at once. He looked at her in silence for a moment, and she understood for the first time that the strangely dark expression in his radiant eyes told of a hunger that made her heart beat fast because she knew that hunger sought to devour *her*. "Darling, you must try to be a good girl for the sister. You don't want to have another whipping, do you? I'm afraid to say that I'm sure Sister Stone will use her strap if she must."

"Oh, please," Amanda wailed. "Please don't... Mr. Coventry, don't go!"

"I must go, Amanda. It is time for your training to begin. I promise you will understand more, soon."

He stepped toward her, and, to her amazement, kissed her, in front of the porter and the sister, wrapping his arms about her and making her open her mouth to his probing tongue just as he had in the carriage. She had blushed furiously enough in the closed coach; now her face felt as hot as the sun, not only to be kissed that way, outdoors and in front of others, but because she felt her body now give itself up to James even more than it had when their kisses lay hidden from the world's sight.

How could he kiss her that way, and not promise to marry her? Instead of receiving a proposal, Miss Amanda Eaker must, it seemed, now undress in the spring air of what it seemed would soon become a lovely Westmoreland morning. Even if she did not receive another whipping, from this terrible Sister Stone, the sister would see the marks from her erstwhile suitor's strap, whose lingering smart, Amanda felt, had somehow led to some large part of the confused emotions she now felt about James and the queer college to which he had brought her.

"Goodbye, darling," James said softly, after he had broken the long kiss. He held her at arms' length and turned her toward the sister. "Be a good girl for me, now." He gave her a little push, gentle but definite, and Amanda could not help taking a fearful step forward.

"I'm sure she will, sir," Sister Stone said to James. "Turn around, child, and I'll unhook you. No fuss for me now. You have a fine gentleman, and you will make him a fine bedmate, soon enough."

As she allowed herself to be turned by the nursing sister's strong hands, she watched James follow the porter inside the house. She couldn't help a little sob when she felt Sister Stone's fingers begin to unhook her simple blue calico gown.

"Weep as much as you like, so long as you don't give me any trouble, girl," the woman said.

"But I don't understand!" Amanda said again, her hands balling into fists of outraged modesty. "What is this place? Why… why must I undress this way?"

"Hush, now, miss. 'Tis a place girls must enter naked, and that's all you need to know at present."

CHAPTER EIGHT

Dr. Brown examined Miss Amanda Eaker at four o'clock. Until that time, according to the doctor's protocol for the admission of new girls, Amanda had remained, naked and of course under close observation, in her cell. Sister Stone had brought her breakfast and then, after Amanda had slept a while upon the comfortable bed, a simple dinner of meat and potatoes.

The cells of the College for Advanced Study truly only deserved that name for their general configuration: only six feet wide and ten feet long and possessed of a single window placed too high in the wall for the vast majority of young women to see out. The comfortable bed itself was of a greater width than one would ordinarily find in such a room, however, in order to permit a man to have coitus easily with the cell's inmate. A thick Persian rug lay upon the floor, and an oil lamp, standing on a table next to the bed, shed a warm light.

In this cell Mr. Coventry would deflower Miss Eaker not long after her initial examination. She did not of course know this fact yet, and the first hours she spent there gave Dr. Brown nearly as much important information about her case as the examination itself would.

Deprived of her clothing and in a strange room whose more cell-like aspects could not but stir thoughts and even fantasies of dungeons and gaols, Miss Eaker must contemplate why her savior had decreed a residence in such a place.

"That's a well-punished bottom," Sister Stone had said, after making the girl bend over the bed for an initial inspection. Dr. Brown observed through the peephole let into every cell door. "You'll want to touch it, miss, I'm sure, but that's forbidden right now. So is touching between your legs, of course." The nursing sister's hands roved over the shapely little bottom with its delicate tracery of marks from the strap. Miss Eaker whimpered.

"Are you wet, child?" asked Sister Stone softly, skillfully beginning what Dr. Brown called the *priming* process.

Miss Eaker could render only the least articulate of responses, as the sister's fingers sought out the answer.

"You certainly are wet, aren't you?" the older woman said insinuatingly. "That's just fine. You're ashamed now, I know, but you are here to learn that you must lose that false modesty when it suits your gentleman for you to lose it. When I shave your vulva later, it will help you understand."

A sob came from Miss Eaker's throat as Sister Stone continued her manual inspection, undoubtedly stimulating the clitoris directly for just a moment before she removed her hands and dried them on her apron.

"Hop into bed, now, child. There is a bun and a glass of milk for you there on the table. I shall return in a few hours with dinner, and you shall see the doctor after that."

"M-must I be… *naked* the whole time?" Miss Eaker asked plaintively.

"Of course," the sister replied, as if the question were absurd. "New girls are always naked. After you have learned to please the cocksmen, the doctor may allow you to wear clothes again sometimes, but that won't be for days and days at least."

From his station outside the cell, Dr. Brown had a very

clear view of the way Miss Eaker, in the act of climbing into bed and obviously relieved to have at least the bedclothes to cover her nudity, dropped her jaw without having a single thing to say. The account he had received from Mr. Coventry over breakfast, of Miss Eaker's encounter with her would-be bridegroom the previous afternoon, indicated that the 'gentleman' farmer had demystified coitus for the girl somewhat. The doctor's knowledge of human nature, too, made him feel quite sure that words like *cock*, *cunt*, and *fuck*, now made a part of Miss Eaker's passive vocabulary. Many new girls, on hearing the term *cocksmen*, would think of roosters—but Miss Eaker's face showed that her priming continued apace.

Accordingly, she did not fall asleep for a long while, after finishing her simple breakfast. While Dr. Brown watched patiently, she turned upon her side, after finding it uncomfortable for her bottom to be upon her back, and her hands dutifully outside the counterpane. She gazed at them fixedly, as if willing herself to stop wishing to do what Sister Stone had told her she must not do.

Dr. Brown wrote in his notebook, on the page newly reserved for Case 35,

Miss Eaker a good girl. Masturbation a temptation, but easily regulated at this stage.

When, upon waking the girl at two o'clock, Sister Stone had made her stoop upon the chamber pot under the sister's watchful eye, so that Miss Eaker turned bright red at the sound of her urine hissing into the porcelain, Dr. Brown wrote,

Significant shame surrounding bodily functions: normal.

When, after Miss Eaker had dinner, the sister made her sit upon a towel, then lie back and spread her legs for shaving, and the girl demanded, in tears but also in vain, to know why she must be shaved, the doctor wrote,

Miss Eaker's vulva exceptionally tidy; her anus currently tight and attractive. Advise Coventry that he has something of value in that area.

In the wake of Dr. Brown's essay, an amusing sort of trade had sprung up among the work's admirers: since one of the doctor's tenets was that natural men should have no qualms about sharing and even selling the favors of the girls over whom they exercised their natural rights, auctions were held on a near-monthly basis for the display and hiring of such charms as pretty vaginas and anuses.

"All you need know, miss," the sister said in a more soothing tone than was usual with her—proving that Miss Amanda Eaker had certain powers of attraction that would have to be taken into account in her treatment—"is that the doctor wishes you to be bare down here, for the sake of your treatment and your training." She had nearly finished with the shaving, now, and was removing a few hairs in Miss Eaker's anal area with tweezers, provoking little yelps from the girl. "I told you this morning that not having your grownup hair here will help you learn to let go of your modesty, for your gentleman, and that's all I can say."

After that, Dr. Brown went to wake Mr. Coventry, and found him—as the doctor suspected he would—already awake and waiting for the summons to the examination room. When the newest of the college's cocksmen first beheld Dr. Brown's modern examination table, custom-made of oak, with leather straps in case of the necessity of immobilizing a girl for her own good, he frowned, as they all did.

"Miss Eaker will lie upon the table and put her knees into these supports," the doctor said patiently, pointing to the two well-padded, crutch-like spreaders (as Dr. Brown called them privately). "I'll ask you to strap her knees in, if necessary, while I put the belt around her waist, but that probably won't be required. I can already tell your young lady is a good girl. Go ahead and take off your own clothing, please."

"I say!" said Mr. Coventry. "I didn't think…"

The doctor smiled, well used to this initial reluctance on the part of a new cocksman. "Mr. Coventry," he said, "I am not insensible of the value of female nudity counter-posed to male dress, and I assure you that in future parts of your Miss Eaker's treatment and training you will remain clothed while she is naked."

The younger man frowned, very intelligently Dr. Brown thought. The liking he had developed almost instantly for James Coventry on meeting him in London found confirmation in the man's obvious thoughtfulness. "You do say, in your essay, that when possible, a girl who is to be possessed should be stripped bare of those appurtenances of shame thrust upon her by society…"

"Such as her corset and her petticoats and even her shift and drawers," the doctor affirmed, letting his approval of Mr. Coventry's close study of the essay be heard in his tone, "while the man who will exercise his natural erotic rights upon her should demonstrate insofar as possible that he may keep those appurtenances on if he prefers. Indeed, but do you remember, Mr. Coventry, that I write elsewhere that the *membrum virile* must be shown plainly to a girl who will be trained, in order that she may develop a sense of her own natural desire to please it, along with hearing her master's clear command that to receive his penis is her most important task?"

Mr. Coventry nodded thoughtfully. "And I am to give that command to Miss Eaker here and now?"

"Indeed yes. You say she has had that other man's penis in her mouth already? And been made to swallow his semen?"

The young man nodded.

"Then you shall give her the command while she pleasures you the same way, here in my examination room, while I observe and instruct. It is important that Miss Eaker

sees very clearly into what sort of new life she has come—
that is one of the most important purposes of our
examination here today. At the same time, she will begin to
develop the close acquaintance with your penis that will help
her learn to please you as you have the natural right to
expect."

Mr. Coventry nodded one final time, and turned away to
begin undressing. Dr. Brown smiled a little ruefully and
shook his head gently at the young man's lingering modesty.
Most cocksmen instinctively did the same thing when told
to strip themselves naked the first few times. Intellectually
they all knew that the doctor would see their penises as soon
as they turned around, and then would see them use those
penises in the instructional activities in which he requested
they engage with their girls. Just as it took those girls several
weeks of training to ride the masturbation saddle without
protest or spread their bottom cheeks for anal coitus the
moment they were told to do so, the gentlemen needed time
to adjust to a life where modesty represented a strategy and
a tool rather than an existential necessity.

When handsome James Coventry, having one of the
larger penises Dr. Brown had ever seen, did turn around,
the doctor picked up the bell on his desk and rang it.
Instantly the door opened, and Sister Stone led Miss Eaker
into the room. Mr. Coventry, seeing a shaved girl for the
first time, swallowed hard but kept his composure. Miss
Eaker, seeing a naked man for the first time—and of course
despite being herself naked—gave a little cry of surprise and
cowered back.

The doctor noted dispassionately that Mr. Coventry's
already sizable penis had grown somewhat.

"Miss Eaker," he said, "I am Dr. Brown. I am very happy
to meet you."

The girl looked at him with wide eyes and red face.

"Sister, you may go. I'll ring again when it's time to take
Miss Eaker back to her cell."

"Yes, Doctor," said Sister Stone. "Be a good girl, miss,"

she said, and receded through the door, closing it behind her.

The doctor turned back to Miss Eaker. "There is no use in my trying to pretend, young lady, that the purposes for which Mr. Coventry has brought you to my college would be called anything but terribly shameful by the vast majority of the civilized world. Today, with his help, I shall begin to reconcile you to those purposes, for which I assure you your body was made, just as his was made—as you can see—to enjoy your youthful charms. You sucked a penis yesterday, I understand?"

Miss Eaker made no immediate answer. She had moved back, hands over breasts and vulva, until her backside touched the wall of the little room. Her jaw hung open, and her breath came in short pants.

Dr. Brown looked at Mr. Coventry, eyebrows raised, and the young man took the suggestion.

"Tell Dr. Brown what you told me, darling," he said. "A man named Charlton whipped her until she would take his penis in her mouth. He made her suck until he spent, and she had to swallow his seed."

The doctor looked in a kindly way at Miss Eaker. "Is that right, Miss Eaker? You mustn't be ashamed, for you are going to do the same thing for Mr. Coventry now."

CHAPTER NINE

James could scarcely believe how hard his cock had gotten at the sight of Miss Amanda Eaker with no hair upon her cunt. A moment before, he had begun to doubt whether, despite the intellectual assent he had given Dr. Brown's essay and the envy he had felt of the erotic happiness bestowed upon the Scotsman's *proven natural men* in the exercise of their erotic rights, his own education would stand in the way of James Coventry, Esq. becoming one of them. He had hesitated to undress in front of the doctor, and then he had turned away to do so, as absurd as he knew the gesture to be.

But his prick stood now at full attention, as it had done the moment Amanda came in and James saw that they had shaved her between her legs. Even with Sister Stone still in the room, James Coventry, Esq.'s penis leapt into hardness and he felt no need to cover himself, to hide it. Amanda would see what he had for her, and she would suck it like a good girl.

The genius of Dr. Brown appeared to him already in this idea: he could not deny that all yesterday, simply thinking of what Lord Rider had given Mr. Charlton leave to do—to make Amanda suck his prick, and to whip her if she proved reluctant—had stirred envy and jealousy such as he had never known. When he saw her come toward him from the shadow the barn, and understood that she must be walking stiffly because Charlton had indeed used his strap upon her, and that that must mean he had also possessed her sweet young mouth until he filled it with his seed, a quiet rage suffused him that had not departed even as he'd kissed the girl he had so clearly won away from the dolt to whom the baron had given her.

Now, James' cock would be the one to thrust inside Miss Amanda Eaker's mouth, and James' semen would be her afternoon beverage. What better way to make it clear to both of them what man would henceforward be her lord and master? When he added to that thought the delicious new impression of how bare they had made Amanda's cunt for her studies at the College of Advanced Study—the way the hint of tender cleft between her thighs showed James the way to the delights he would soon find hidden there—he had not a doubt left in him.

"Answer the doctor's question, Amanda," he said a little sternly. "Or you shall have to be whipped again."

James glanced at Dr. Brown to see if the man approved, feeling that he did it out of curiosity rather than any need to please another where his conduct toward his naked young lady was concerned. The doctor's nod gratified his pride nevertheless, and confirmed James in his sense that he would continue to discover within himself the natural man. As the doctor had written, he would lift himself by his own bootstraps, with assistance from the curriculum of the college: to master Amanda seemed now simply a matter of letting his primal instincts guide him.

Amanda looked up at him with a woeful pout on her face, then, as if she could not have helped it even if her village schoolmistress had been there holding a ruler, her eyes went down to his hard penis. Again James let his dominant nature guide him. He smiled.

"This is *my* cock, darling," he said. He took it in his left hand and pumped it gently. "You have gotten it very hard."

"*I* have?!" Amanda whispered with an urgency that belied the softness of the words. "I don't... I don't understand!" She looked desperately at Dr. Brown, as if in hope that he would explain, and that his explanation would also put a stop to the scene that stirred such troubled feelings in her breast and much further down, where James suddenly felt sure, she must be warm and wet.

"Yes," the doctor said, "in the most important sense, Miss Eaker, you have caused Mr. Coventry's penis to become erect. A natural man like your gentleman here grows aroused at the prospect of possessing a girl he has taken under his care, especially when she is naked, and the places of his enjoyment begin to be revealed to him. You probably didn't notice, either when you were made to take a penis in your mouth the first time, yesterday, or today when you arrived here in the examination room, that the male penis is actually in a resting, or flaccid, state most of the time. Once you have fellated Mr. Coventry—we call the act of yielding the mouth to the penis' pleasure *fellatio*, the old Roman word for it—and brought him to climax, as I understand you did for Mr. Charlton? Is that right, Miss Eaker? Did Mr. Charlton ejaculate inside your mouth? That's a doctor's word for emitting seminal fluid, which you would probably have found thick and perhaps a little bitter."

James watched Amanda's face closely as she listened to the Scotsman's bland articulation of matters that had always lain for her—James felt sure—under a veil of secrecy so impenetrable that the very idea that men and women might do the same sorts of things farm girls and boys inevitably saw the animals do had not occurred to her. She had probably heard some confused version of these things from the friend who had had to marry Mr. Penny, but this medical explanation seemed at once to soothe and to shock her.

Realizing a little belatedly that Dr. Brown had posed again the question of what Mr. Charlton had done to her the previous afternoon, Amanda nodded slowly.

"I imagine he buttoned himself up immediately and went away, after he ejaculated in your mouth?"

"Y-yes," the lovely naked girl stammered.

"Quite," the doctor said, nodding and making a note in his little notebook. "Well, as I was saying, once Mr. Coventry has climaxed and ejaculated, you will be able to watch his penis become flaccid. Then, a few minutes after that, you will certainly see it grow erect again, in response to his arousal at the prospect of enjoying himself inside your vagina, which he will do for the first time this evening. Kneel in front of him now, if you please, and he will insert his penis in your mouth. I imagine you will find him gentler than Mr. Charlton, though here at my college you will also learn to receive his deepest thrusting, when he chooses to employ your oral cavity that way, as a sort of analogue of your vagina."

But Amanda shook her head slowly, looking from Dr. Brown to James and back. She swallowed hard, and very visibly.

James stepped forward, his arms open. Amanda's eyes grew wide, but though she could have shrunk further against the wall, she didn't, but merely trembled as he took her in his arms for their first naked embrace. The feeling of her bare skin, of her little breasts against his abdomen with their tiny nipples erect with the arousal he could tell—instinctively, again—she felt, lifted his senses into a realm of erotic anticipation of which he had scarcely dreamt.

Amanda gave a little whimper, and then a long sigh, as she relaxed in his arms just as she had in the carriage, when her blue calico and her corset and petticoats, drawers and shift, had still covered her. "You must, darling," James said softly, knowing in his mind, in his heart, and indeed in his scrotum, that to instruct her in that way constituted one of his most important roles as her cocksman.

"Yes," she whispered, into his naked chest.

James looked down and saw her eyes upturned to his, and when their gazes met, Amanda began to sink down within his embrace. He helped her, feeling the way the dominant gesture and the thought of the pleasure that would now belong to him made his cock leap. He pushed her gently to the floor as she yielded herself to that fundamental gesture of submission.

Amanda looked up, as if for instructions, but James said, "Eyes on my cock, darling. Open your mouth."

A hint of a blush came to her cheeks as she obeyed. James beheld the terribly moving sight of his sweet, golden-haired young lady, naked before him on her knees, with the head of his cock hovering only an inch from her nose and her open mouth.

"Wait a moment," said Dr. Brown from behind him. "Mr. Coventry, it is of course up to you, but it's advisable to allow Miss Eaker to touch your penis at this point, with her hands, and to become acquainted with it. The foundation of your pleasure in her submission will henceforth be her eagerness to serve your penis, rather than her fear either of the coitus you rightly demand or of what you will do if she does not obey."

The blush upon Amanda's face grew deeper.

"There will of course be times when you must discipline her not only for faults in her conduct such as laziness or speaking out of turn but also for faults in her submission such as looking you in the eye without permission during coitus. But the grave error into which unnatural men such as Mr. Charlton fall is to suppose that it is right that a girl should fear them. When you punish Miss Eaker, strange as it may seem to both of you now, you will make her happy despite the tears the rod brings for that little while she must have it upon her bare bottom."

James frowned as he continued to look down at Amanda, his hands resting lightly on her shoulders. He had felt a slight pang of conscience at the way the thought of punishing his young lady made his cock leap again, but much to his surprise he thought he could hear in her breathing a corresponding response from her at the same notion. Dr. Brown knew what he was about, it seemed.

"Neither of you will fully understand what I am telling you, of course. Here at the College of Advanced Study we believe above all in learning through experience, and through practice. You will begin this practice now, and I merely ask you to bear in mind what I have just said."

The doctor fell silent, and James considered, very briefly, then cast his eye quickly about him and found a chair against the wall to his right, and before it a little pillow that he had not noticed earlier. Confident that he knew the purpose of chair and pillow exactly, he said gently to Amanda, "You will kiss my cock, and then we will go over to the chair, so you may learn to please me."

Her eyes darted up to his, and then immediately down again as if the stern expression on his face recalled to her his command to look only at his cock. Her blush, which had ebbed at the doctor's last words, surged back full force.

James took his cock again in his left hand, and, feeling like a king receiving the only tribute that mattered to him, he held it right before Amanda's lips. Pleased at the sight, he watched a drop of the transparent precursor fluid appear in the tiny eye.

"Oh!" Amanda exclaimed, her eyebrows going up. "What is that?" She seemed not alarmed, but perhaps even a little pleased at the thought that the strange thing had happened because of her.

James wondered for a moment whether Dr. Brown would intervene with a medical explanation, but he seemed to regard his role in such a moment of *practice* to be more retiring. James thought he could understand why: the chief source of a girl's knowledge about her master's pleasure should be that natural man's own mind and words.

"That is a sort of liquor that comes before my seed does. Along with your spittle it will ease my way inside you."

"It will not harm me?"

Amanda's face had such a fascinated expression upon it now that James said gently, "Look into my eyes, darling."

She did, a little fearfully now. He smiled. "I will never harm you, especially with my cock."

She smiled back, and the blush receded—and then, to James' delight returned, as if she had just thought of something naughty. Her lips twitched, and she returned her attention to his cock unbidden, as he pumped it slowly in his hand.

"Does it feel good," she asked, "to rub it like that?"

"Very good, darling," he said. "Now kiss my cock, and I will anoint your lips with that liquor. Then you shall kneel upon the pillow, and you may play with your master's cock as you like, and show me what a good girl you can be."

CHAPTER TEN

Master. Had James truly said 'master'? Like a schoolmaster: a man who took charge of you, and taught you.

But how could a master teach a girl this sort of lesson? Amanda felt her brow crease as she looked at the long, hard thing in her master's hand, with the strange little eye, almost like a tiny buttonhole, at the end, where the drop of *liquor* seemed to grow in size a little as James rubbed.

She must kiss it, must she not? She had had to let Mr. Charlton put his own cock in her mouth, and move it until the seed came—should that not mean that when her angel instructed her to kiss *his* cock, Amanda must obey? Should she not wish to kiss her angel's—her mastering angel's—cock, knowing that she must have her bare bottom whipped again if she refused?

That made the trouble, though, didn't it? James had told her he would punish her if she disobeyed, but Amanda knew from the way he kissed her, the way he held her, that such punishment would be a terribly different thing from Mr. Charlton's strap. This strange Dr. Brown had confirmed that difference with his words: Miss Amanda Eaker would receive regular discipline here at the doctor's college and,

66

presumably, afterward, but her thrashings would be of a nature not to make her fear her shameful duty but rather to love it.

How could she love it? How could she *want* to kiss the thing James held in front of her face, the same sort of thing Mr. Charlton had moved in and out, murmuring, "Is this what bad girls get, Amanda Eaker? Will you suck the prick like a good wife, or must I whip you every time?"

But… she *did* want to kiss it, though she knew she shouldn't. Then, though: the pillow, and the touching, and the sucking. Amanda couldn't want to have *that* kind of lesson, could she? These were the parts of his body, and her body, that no one should see or talk about. To have *lessons* about them would surely bring down the wrath of the constabulary, or the church, or the queen, would it not?

Then: her vagina, which must be the same thing Mr. Charlton had called her *cunt* and her *cunny*, must it not? The awful man had said he would *fuck* her there—and now Dr. Brown said James, her angel, would soon do the same thing. *Coitus*, he called it. *Coitus* must mean James putting his cock inside her and moving it back and forth until he spurted his seed from the tip.

The thoughts in her mind had come to such a jumble now that Amanda wanted to cry. She looked at the hard penis, and she knew she must learn to please Mr. James Coventry, and she knew she must not look him in the eye but must look only at this lordly, arrogant, upright part of him.

"Kiss, darling," came his voice from above. "Kiss the cock."

Amanda leaned forward, her heart beating very fast and her breath coming in short gasps through her nostrils as she pursed her lips. James' right hand cupped the back of her neck very gently, so unlike the way Mr. Charlton had held her face in place, and he moved his hips very slightly, so that the tip of his penis did touch her lips at last.

She gave a little whimper of surprise and submission at

how soft he felt there, and how wicked the liquor felt upon her lips. Amanda realized with shame that the shaved place between her thighs had grown warm at the first touch of her master's penis.

"Good girl," James said softly. Suddenly Amanda wanted to please him so much that her jaw fell open automatically; something about how eager Mr. Charlton had been to thrust his cock inside her there, and how pleasant it had seemed to him to possess her that way despite the terrible shame for her, made her feel that she must do that for her angel right now, and let him, too, enjoy himself inside her mouth.

But James said, "Over to the pillow, darling," and he raised her up and held her close again for a moment, their naked embrace sending the same shivery thrill through Amanda's body as it had when first he enfolded her thus, before he pushed her down to her knees to serve him. He led her the few feet to the pillow, covered in a strong undyed twill, which lay before the big leather armchair.

"Kneel down, now," James said, and Amanda obeyed.

He sat in the chair, and his cock rose up so tall that Amanda blushed again. For the first time she noticed that he also had something down below, like a tight little purse, very wrinkly and full perhaps of some fluid. Full of his seed? Her blush grew hotter. The stiff, curly brown hair James had between his legs reminded Amanda of course that she no longer had her own nether tresses: she had known, the previous morning, that men's bodies differed from girls', but it seemed that part of her curriculum here at the College of Advanced Study would reinforce that distinction even more greatly than nature itself already had.

"You may touch your cocksman's penis and his scrotum, Miss Eaker, and you may ask questions if you like." The doctor's voice came from behind her, and Amanda realized she had somehow forgotten about his presence.

"Scrotum?" she whispered, though she already guessed to what the word must refer.

James took his hard penis in his hand and moved it aside and up so that she could see the little purse better. "This is my scrotum, darling; it holds my balls—my testes, the doctor would say. Kiss it and touch it very gently. It will give me pleasure."

The aroma that rose to her nose from her *cocksman's*— she wanted to ask about that word, too, but she didn't have the courage—loins seemed wicked, earthy... the kind of smell that only naughty girls must smell. As she bent to obey and kiss the strange little sack, it seemed to overwhelm her senses, so that when James sighed and his hands came gently around her head again as if to hold her to him in that shameful place, it all whirled around too fast in her mind even to comprehend, and she started to struggle.

But James, as if himself overcome by desire for the pleasure his young lady could give, said, "Open your mouth, now, Amanda."

She obeyed, and somehow obeying made her stop trying to get away, and now he had moved her mouth upward and put the cock inside it. "There," he said, in a voice that seemed to betray such pleasure with her that she tried to move her mouth up and down upon the thing that filled her so full there.

"Use your hands as well, Miss Eaker," said Dr. Brown. "Up and down just as Mr. Coventry did to himself. When a girl can't yet take the penis all the way inside her mouth, her hands will help greatly."

Amanda did use her hands, wonderingly, suddenly understanding that she—Miss Amanda Eaker—had a good deal more control over her cocksman's pleasure than she had thought she would.

"How is she progressing, Mr. Coventry?" Dr. Brown asked.

"Very... very... well," James replied huskily, and Amanda, suddenly restored to her wits and her senses, heard him grip the armrests of the chair so tight the wood creaked.

With her right hand she pumped gently up and down at

the base of the shaft, sensing that he liked that, while with her left she ventured to hold the scrotum gently, as she moved her mouth up and down, growing surer from her angelic master's bodily responses that she had indeed progressed quickly. She pictured herself for a moment as he must see her, kneeling naked before him like a Greek nymph or a seductive fairy in a storybook, doing the sort of thing the stories never referred to but which—Amanda thought suddenly—must have happened for all those heroes to run around slaying things.

The image made her blush, but together with the idea that *she* could *choose* how to please him, Amanda knew she could learn how to do it better and better. She knew, too, that she wanted to learn how, with Mr. James Coventry as her master.

His hands returned to her head, as if the pleasure she had given had grown so great he must still her upon his cock. He twined his right hand in her hair, as he had when he kissed her in the carriage, and stroked her cheek with his left, and then his hips came up off the cushion of his chair and the hot seed was spurting into Amanda's mouth. To her amazement, it tasted different from Mr. Charlton's, and she wondered whether she imagined that difference—certainly if she had said Mr. Coventry's seed tasted angelic, she would be dishonest, but she found it much easier to obey him when he murmured, "Swallow it, darling. Every bit in your tummy for me."

Then he said, "You pleased me very much indeed, Miss Eaker. You may look into my face."

She did, finding that a shy smile had come upon her lips, which felt besmirched but somehow, now, lovely in that besmirching. He smiled down at her and stroked her cheek.

Dr. Brown said, "Observe what happens now to Mr. Coventry's penis. It has already grown much softer, and soon it will be quite flaccid. Do not touch it for a few moments; a man has a time after he has had his climax in which to be touched there is unpleasant."

So Amanda observed, and indeed the sight seemed very wondrous to her: she understood how men could walk about easily with their penises in their breeches and trousers, something that had been mystifying her after her encounter with Mr. Charlton.

"We shall have you up on my examination table, now, Miss Eaker," the doctor said pleasantly.

Amanda turned to look at the strange article of furniture that she had scarcely noticed upon entering, so greatly had the sight of Mr. Coventry's penis confused her. At first she could not see how the padded surface might accommodate a person even as small in stature as she, and she looked at the Scotsman in puzzlement.

"Just climb up here," he said, patting the table, "and lie upon your back. These supports are for your knees."

Instantly Amanda saw herself upon the thing, in her mind's eye, and her real eyes went wide as the heat came to her face. The 'supports' were so... far apart!

"Go on, darling," James said, stroking her shoulder in what he must mean as a comforting gesture but that felt to her so possessive that she shivered. "I wish to see you that way."

No, he hadn't meant it to comfort her after all, had he? He wanted to see his *young lady*, as the doctor kept calling her, spread out on that table. But he would see *everything*— Mr. Coventry, her mastering angel, and the doctor who seemed to know so much about how to place a young lady in subjection under a cocksman's dominion.

And she? Did she wish him to see her that way? Her most private places, bare now of their adult curls?

No. It would be too shameful. All the things he says I will have to do, to undergo... they are all too shameful. He wants to put his cock inside me there, just as horrid Mr. Charlton said he would do—just as horrid Mr. Penny does to Jane, and in her bottom-hole, too. Jane said it hurt so much, the first time he did it!

But...

She must, must she not? Mr. Coventry wished to see her

that way.

Amanda cast her eyes to the floor, and could not raise them, but she rose, moved to the place where a little footstool stood, and stepped upon it, knowing with another surge of heat in her cheeks that as she climbed up, James would see her bare secrets peeping out. Somehow it didn't matter then that she had decided to obey him, and show him everything when she turned over and spread her legs; the idea that he could see her cunny from behind as she climbed up brought further shame, no matter how illogical it seemed.

"All right, Miss Eaker. Turn over and put your knees up, and let's have a look at you. I'll examine your vagina and anus now, and instruct you now about how Mr. Coventry's penis will change things, down there, when you have first coitus in a little while. We'll also talk about your pleasures, as a young lady, and if Mr. Coventry chooses I'll bring you to your first climax, to prepare you to respond gratefully when the penis is inside you."

CHAPTER ELEVEN

Dr. Brown washed his hands in the washstand and dried them on a towel, as he continued to instruct Miss Eaker.

"The shape of your vagina, Miss Eaker, decreed by nature itself, has as its purpose penetration by the equally natural shape of Mr. Coventry's penis. When your beauty and submission arouse him, he will put his penis there and please himself until he ejaculates his semen into you. Nature has also fashioned other regions of your body to receive the penis, though, and when Mr. Coventry pleases he will enjoy you there also, as of course he just has inside your mouth. His penis has bestowed on him the right to enjoy you, and here at my college you will learn that you must allow him to exercise that right as frequently as he likes, and in whatever manner he prefers at the time."

He looked into the sweet girl's eyes. As she had performed fellatio on Mr. Coventry, the doctor had made several notes, whose purport he now bore closely in mind.

Modesty the principal barrier with Miss Eaker. Experience with unnatural man, of whipping and fellatio, complicates response to natural cocksman, however. Awakening to submissive feminine pleasure indicated soonest, now that she has fellated Mr. C.

Miss Eaker looked back at him with the aspect of a fawn startled in a forest glade.

The doctor turned to Mr. Coventry. "Do you like what you see, sir?"

The cocksman's penis, Dr. Brown noted, swelled a little as he looked at his young lady. The doctor could see that some guilt at stripping away the girl's modesty still lay within the man's mind, however, as he surveyed the charming prospect of the naked eighteen-year-old who had just swallowed his semen and would soon yield up her vagina and anus to his pleasure.

"Yes, Doctor," he said in a very even tone, though. "Very much."

Again Dr. Brown addressed Miss Eaker, who had blushed once again, but also had the ghost of a smile upon her lips at the compliment Mr. Coventry had just paid her.

"Mr. Coventry no doubt remembers the portion of my essay, *On the necessity of men's exercising their masculine rights in erotic matters*, in which I discuss the importance of removing a girl's clothing, or dressing her in scanty garments if he prefers, as an enjoyable prelude to coitus. Especially when a young lady has had the hair upon her vulva removed, the sight of her little body, defenseless and ready for his pleasure, serves as a natural stimulus to his arousal. Do you see how your cocksman's penis has begun to rise again?"

The girl's eyes darted to Mr. Coventry's loins, and the color in her face heightened. She looked back into Dr. Brown's eyes and nodded, her upper lip quivering a little.

"You have begun to fear, a bit, the pain of first coitus?" he said in response to the quiver.

Miss Eaker nodded again.

"That is only natural, when you see the penis that will soon rupture your hymen."

"My what, Doctor?" Miss Eaker whispered.

The doctor smiled. He turned to Mr. Coventry and said, "Look closely, now: most natural men find this sight extremely arousing." Then he turned back to Miss Eaker. "I am going to show your hymen to Mr. Coventry now, and ascertain that your vagina is healthy and ready for coitus."

He reached out and began to palpate the region around the girl's clitoris, then her outer labia, to help her relax and to begin the association of the sight of her master's penis with erotic pleasure. Certainly it did not represent a physician's standard gynecological practice, but Dr. Brown did not pursue conventional results.

"Wh-what are you doing, D-Doctor?" Miss Eaker stammered. But Dr. Brown focused his attention between her legs, where her erogenous zones had already become warm, and now engorged themselves in the female counterpart of male erection.

"Do you see how she responds to my touch, Mr. Coventry? Notice that her own natural liquor, akin to yours, has begun to gather in her vagina, to ease your way when you penetrate her there."

Miss Eaker made whimpering sounds as the palpation continued.

"Remember to pay your principal attention to this shy little bud, as most men call it, at the top." With the fingers of his right hand, the doctor gently spread the hood of pink flesh that concealed the girl's clitoris, and showed her cocksman the most sensitive part of his young lady's body. "Observe what happens when I stimulate the clitoris directly."

With his left forefinger, Dr. Brown softly touched the stiff little nub. Miss Eaker cried out. "Oh!" and then, as the doctor continued, "Oh, heaven... oh, Doctor, please... James, do not..." Her bottom squirmed and her hips moved back and forth as if she sought more of the pleasure the doctor gave her, but in spite of herself.

"Shall I allow Miss Eaker to climax, Mr. Coventry? It is your right to decide."

The girl's head threshed from side to side, and her eyes were closed. She arched her back up off the padded table in pursuit of the pleasure of which she had never dreamed. Her hands, at either side of her belly, gripped the leather padding with their fingertips.

"Of course, Doctor," the man said, as Dr. Brown knew he would.

Miss Eaker gave a sob of gratitude, for she clearly now could feel that a crisis for her body approached: the cliff of her orgasm, which she must either soar over or be turned away in tears.

But the doctor ceased the immediate stimulus of the clitoris, and spread the girl's vagina open for his and her cocksman's inspection. She gasped at the strange feeling.

"Do you see the hymen, Mr. Coventry? When you insert your erect penis for the first time, and thrust it inside fully, as nature will command you to do, you will rupture this membrane, which Hippocrates named after the Greek divinity of marriage, Hymen."

He looked up at Miss Eaker, who had opened her eyes again, her face flushed. "I am afraid, Miss Eaker, that nature made you so that you might not easily behold your own vagina. Although in general I accept the decree of nature, in this case I think it is important that you see how you are made. Soon, too, you will see the vaginas of other girls as well." He reached over to his little desk and took up the hand mirror. He gave it to Mr. Coventry.

"Hold this so that Miss Eaker, too, can look inside her vagina, and also see her anus while I discuss her erotic duties with her."

The younger man accepted the mirror with slightly knitted brows, as if a little surprised that his young lady should be allowed to see a sight so very immodest.

"That's it, Mr. Coventry. Just about there. Do you see, Miss Eaker?"

The girl had started to pant a little, as Dr. Brown accompanied the ceremony of the mirror with a bit of renewed attention to her clitoris. "Yes, Doctor," she whispered.

"Do you see the white membrane inside? That is what most people call the maidenhead—that is, the hymen that we are discussing now."

"That is my maidenhead?" she said in a small voice, as if she had never supposed that a *maidenhead* was anything but a vague metaphor. "And I-I sh-shall *lose* it? Today?"

The doctor smiled. The idea of a girl *losing* her maidenhead held a great significance, both positive and negative, in the minds of the vast majorities of young women educated in England.

"Yes, Miss Eaker. When Mr. Coventry penetrates your vagina with his penis, he will tear though it—rupture is the technical term. There will be a bit of discomfort for you, as you are deflowered—again, according to the common way of speaking—and some blood. Even so, however, you will start to feel some of the pleasure to which I have already aroused you, and which—since Mr. Coventry has permitted it—I will as you might say *perfect* in a few moments."

The young lady swallowed hard. "When... will he...?"

"After tea," the doctor said, "you will be brought back to your cell to think about your new life as Mr. Coventry's young lady, and your service to his sexual needs. He will come to you there, have first coitus with you, and then probably have coitus several more times in the night, waking you as he chooses to enjoy your vagina again. He will not have anal intercourse with you tonight, but tomorrow night you must expect that he will do so, as is right, and Sister Stone will give you a lesson in the afternoon, on how to present your buttocks and anus for his penis."

A deep crease had appeared on Miss Eaker's brow as she heard this information, and now she bit her lip. The doctor had continued to stimulate her gently as he spoke, placing a delicate finger on her anus when he mentioned anal intercourse and working it inside a bit so that the girl understood that a natural man had the right to introduce into her rectum what he chose.

Now he reached over again to his desk and fetched the

speculum. He showed it to Miss Eaker. "This is a gynecological speculum. At your next examination, I shall use it inside your vagina, but until Mr. Coventry has had first coitus with you and ruptured your hymen, the danger of depriving him of that pleasure is too great. Some men have said that girls' hymens should simply be ruptured in their physicians' offices, but as you have seen I hold as much as possible with the dictates of nature. Nature decreed that you, Miss Eaker, should have your maidenhead taken by the man who has won you."

The girl chewed upon her inner cheek now, instead of biting her lip, but the frown of mingled shame and arousal remained.

"On the other hand, I will put my speculum in your rectum and examine you there, both to ascertain your health and to give you a preliminary lesson in relaxing your anal musculature, as you must do when it is time for Mr. Coventry to put his erect penis there. Mr. Coventry, if you move a bit, you will be able to show Miss Eaker what I am doing, which should prove instructive to both of you."

Dr. Brown took a little jelly from the jar on his desk on his fingers and smeared it over the beak of the speculum. Then, as Miss Eaker gave a little cry at the feeling, the sight in the mirror, or both, he inserted the speculum in her rectum and began to open it.

"Oh, Doctor, please…" she moaned.

"Try to relax, Miss Eaker," he replied. "I am opening your sphincter muscle, as it is called, a little wider than Mr. Coventry's penis will open it. His vigorous motions, however, will prove something of an ordeal at first, during anal coitus. Mr. Coventry, she looks just fine in here, and you may have frequent anal intercourse with her. Sister Stone will keep her clean for you; the girls get frequent enemas both to keep them docile and to make sure they're ready when a cocksman wants to enjoy an anus."

"Oh, no…" Amanda whispered, undoubtedly conversant with the idea of an enema from her life upon her father's farm.

As he withdrew the speculum from her backside, Dr. Brown said, "Don't worry, Miss Eaker, all the girls come to enjoy their enemas greatly. Sister Stone will occasionally administer a disciplinary enema, of course, but if you're a good girl you won't have one of those."

He spoke without looking up from her vagina, where he now began again to rub her adorable little clitoris.

"Observe, Mr. Coventry, how the mention of the enema seems to have increased Miss Eaker's arousal. Also watch the way her muscles are spasming, and above all the bucking of her hips. Miss Eaker, try to restrain yourself a bit, or we shall have to strap you to the table for your own safety."

These words—as the doctor had suspected they might—sent Miss Amanda Eaker soaring over the orgasmic cliff. She looked at Mr. Coventry and reached her hand out for his, which he took, his own eyes darting between the arousing sight of the doctor masturbating his young lady and the lovelier, more ambiguous sight of her entreating eyes. Those beautiful orbs closed now, and the girl moved her buttocks shamelessly upon the table, seeking as much of the pleasure of her first climax as she could have, until she gave a single, piercing cry and lay back, exhausted.

Dr. Brown leaned over to Mr. Coventry and said in his ear, "Praise her."

The young man nodded once, and said with the words clearly ready to his tongue, "Such a good girl, Amanda. Such a good girl, darling, to spend for me that way."

CHAPTER TWELVE

As Sister Stone put Amanda to bed in her cell, the nurse said, "You must prepare yourself well, now, girl. Your gentleman will be with you soon, to have his natural rights."

Amanda felt she should know the answer to the question she asked, then, because she felt that Dr. Brown had given her the key to the mystery of his college's purpose in his examination room. But that time with the doctor and with James had confused her very greatly—not just in the way the doctor kept saying so many wise and complicated things that Amanda knew she wouldn't be able to remember them all, but in the way he and James accompanied those things with overwhelming sensations Amanda had never before experienced.

She spoke timidly to the sister, as the woman removed the covers from the bed. "Are natural rights like *conjugal* rights?"

"Yes and no, my dear, yes and no," the nurse replied, her voice sounding a little warmer than it yet had when addressing Amanda, as if Amanda's respectful question had won some favor with the sister who it appeared now held responsibility over her. "But hush, now, lie down on the bed, and prepare yourself. Think about your gentleman, about his penis, and how hard it will get before he puts it inside you. Make up your mind to be a good girl for him, from the very start. The doctor and your gentleman will tell you much more about natural rights as your training continues."

So Amanda got upon the wide bed—almost as wide as a bed in which two might lie—expecting that Sister Stone would put the covers over her and tuck her into them. The nurse must have seen her looking at the top sheet and counterpane she now held in her slightly gnarled hands.

"Oh, no, dear," she said. "No bedclothes now that might get in the way of your gentleman. You lie there and think about what I told you." She folded the broad fabric she held quickly and efficiently, and put those covers that now covered nothing into the little wardrobe that stood in the corner next to the door.

Sister Stone turned to Amanda one final time. "When I see you again, my dear, you will be a woman. You have a fine gentleman to keep you—very fine indeed. Don't fuss, or be missish about his pleasure and how he likes to have you. You must give him his way, and have his penis inside you as often as he wants to have you tonight. If he likes your vagina so much that he makes you very sore down there, it's a sign that your beauty has captivated him."

Amanda, naked atop the bed, could only stare at the nurse wide-eyed in response to this speech, which went along in perfect harmony with what the doctor had said but seemed somehow even more embarrassing coming from a middle-aged woman.

After Sister Stone had closed the door behind her, Amanda turned upon her side, instinctively covering herself with her hands. She gazed up to where the last of the day's light filtered in through the high window.

Natural rights must be like conjugal rights, mustn't they? They decreed that a man could put his cock inside a girl, it appeared, just as he chose. Amanda didn't feel she could be sure exactly how she knew that in the world of Mrs. Bates, village schoolmistress, a husband's cock only went into his wife's cunny—whether from a softly spoken lesson Amanda had pushed down under the surface of her waking memory, or simply from the consistent, righteous shape of every lesson she had had either from Mrs. Bates or from her own mother—but she felt sure that the idea that the husband instead could make his wife serve his cock in any way he pleased would strike Mrs. Bates as monstrous.

And yet Jane had to have Mr. Penny's cock in her bottom, and so would Amanda, with Mr. Coventry, because of men's right to do that, whether *conjugal* or *natural*.

But… *conjugal* meant *marital*, didn't it? It struck Amanda that there must be an important difference. What did the vicar say at weddings, "for the getting of children"? One thing a farm girl knew is that children came from the womb, out what Dr. Brown had so recently taught Amanda to call the *vagina*. The *cunny*. The *cunt*.

For a husband to say, as Mr. Penny said to Jane and Mr. Charlton had promised to Amanda, that he would make regular use, for his pleasure, of mouth and bottom, *fucking* her in those places just as he did in her cunt, for the getting of children… that couldn't be conjugal, could it?

She thought, suddenly and irresistibly, of James' cock. Of how it had tasted so manly when she had to suck it, kneeling before him. Of how she had been able to make him feel so lovely that the seed had spurted out, which she must swallow even though it didn't taste good. Of how he would put it, long and hard, into her tender little maiden cunny. Of how the sister had shaved Amanda's cunny, because James wanted to see it that way.

Natural. Was natural the *opposite* of conjugal, then? Did Mr. Penny and Mr. Charlton mean 'natural' when they said 'conjugal'?

James wanted to put his cock in her bottom. Dr. Brown said he might do it frequently. James had a big, hard cock that Amanda's body had to receive, wherever he wanted to put it. Amanda's poor cunny. Amanda's poor bottom. She must prepare herself.

She touched herself with her right hand, from behind, between her thighs and between her bottom-cheeks where the welts of Mr. Charlton's strap still felt a little sore. She moved the fingertips gently in and out, up and down, pretending that someone else—James—did it. If someone else did it, it must not be forbidden.

But the little bud at the top... she must not touch herself there, no matter how much she wanted to. When Sister Stone had said that touching herself was forbidden, she must have meant that place, where the doctor had touched to make her have that *spending* thing James had praised her for, that felt so lovely and so shameful at once.

But her cunny was so wet, now. Amanda could slide her fingertips all the way along, move the liquor up, and even put some on the tiny flower of her bottom-hole, which itched a little from the examination, and needed her finger's soothing touch.

She bit her lip, and at first made no sound except the puffs of breath through her nostrils as she grew more excited. Then, though she had no intention of making the little noises, tiny whimpers began to rise from her chest and emerge softly into the air, like the mewling of a kitten. Somehow, to hear those naughty sounds made her feel naughty, and though she had resolved she must not touch the little bud, the *clitoris*, that resolution vanished in a moment. Amanda licked her lips, felt the deep furrow in her brow, and delicately rubbed the most sensitive spot of all.

The kitten whimper grew loud and long, and her hips bucked involuntarily against her hand. She knew how bad a girl she was being, no matter whether she touched herself in front or behind, and so she used her left hand to play with her breasts, and the whimper became a little cry, and she was so close, shockingly close to that wonderful bursting of the ever-expanding bubble inside her tummy, down so low. Just a few more strokes of her fingertips... just a few more.

The door opened. Amanda's hands flew, almost of their

own accord, to the sides, and balled into little fists of surprise and confusion.

"Amanda," James said, stepping into the room in a dressing gown of black damask silk that made him look like a king, or a sorcerer, in a fairytale, "what are you doing?"

Her heart pounded in her chest, and her mouth opened to reply, but no sound came out.

"You may as well know that I have been watching you masturbate, darling, through the peephole in the door," he said, with a sternness in his voice that made her cower a little, curling up on her side and putting her right hand back where it had been, but now to cover herself so that he might not see her cunny.

"Masturbate?" she asked in a whisper.

"Touch your cunt to make yourself feel good."

Amanda swallowed hard.

James parted the dressing gown, then, and took his already hard cock in his hand. "Or, for a man, to do this," he said, demonstrating the same motion he had employed in the doctor's examination room. "Men may masturbate. Girls may not, without special permission."

Something about that made Amanda want to cry, though she couldn't stop watching James' hand go up and down on the shaft of his manhood. Perhaps she knew how lovely he could make himself feel, and the injustice of his interrupting her just as she was feeling the same sort of loveliness seemed almost tragic.

"I think Sister Stone told you not to touch yourself that way—that is, not to masturbate. Is that right?"

Amanda nodded.

"It's my right to punish you for that," James said, and something about the way he said it as he himself masturbated, the head of his cock emerging proudly from his fist with each downward stroke, told Amanda that he *wanted* to punish her—that for some reason it would please him to whip her, just as for some reason, though it seemed lunatic, she *wanted* her angel to whip her. "Or to have the sister do it, or another cocksman, or even to make another of the girls here do it. Discipline is very important here at Dr. Brown's college, and you will be thrashed when you need it."

She had no need to be told to keep her eyes on his penis, now; she saw the little drop of liquor appear, as it had before she kissed the cock for the first time, and suddenly she wanted to kiss again. As he spoke of Amanda's future punishments, his hand seemed to move quicker on his manhood.

How could it make her want to kiss her angel's cock, to hear that she would receive frequent whippings in the house to which he had brought her?

But she said softly, "Yes, sir."

"I must punish you, now, but then I shall give you permission to masturbate in front of me, while you suck my cock. Spread your legs."

So James advanced, and Amanda did as he commanded, spreading her legs so that he could see everything laid out for him, hoping perhaps that to have her that way would appease his wrath. But then, to her dismay, he said, "I shall spank your cunt, darling, because that is where you have committed this offense. Hold your knees open for me."

"Oh, no... sir, please!" Fear rose in her, but at the same time the thought of being punished right *there*, where the naughtiness had started, seemed to stir her so thoroughly that she could not disobey, and she did it, holding herself open though her whole body shook. She watched his hand come up and go down, and she screamed at the terrible agony though the other feeling grew so hot as well. With a rush of heat to her cheeks, she wondered if his hand would come away wet from the cunny he spanked.

She screamed her contrition as he spanked her five times between her legs, and then he said very gently, as if he were sorry to have had to punish her that way, "Now make yourself feel better, darling."

Then he watched her rub the cunny he had spanked,

telling her to put a finger, then two fingers also in her bottom-hole as he steadily moved the cock in her mouth. He stood at the side of the bed and held her head firmly so he could thrust in and out, talking to her of his pleasures all the while.

"The first time I fuck you, in a few moments," he said, "we will fuck face to face, in what is called the matrimonial position. Rub your clitoris now, darling. Very firmly. That's right."

It felt to Amanda much more like James, somehow, touched her through her own fingertips, than that she played with herself, *masturbated*. To touch your cunny with the permission of your angel made that touching, really, not your own—above all when his hard penis thrust in and out of your mouth, at his whim, while you did it.

"Are you going to spend with my cock in your mouth, Amanda? You may do that, if you like. Girls like you can spend over and over, the doctor says, though he says few yet know it."

She did: she spent, crying out around the cock as it used her mouth, and then she did again, when James said, "After I fuck you in the matrimonial position, and you suck me until I have recovered, I will take you from behind, dog-fashion."

CHAPTER THIRTEEN

Watching Amanda play with her sweet, wet cunt as he possessed her mouth, James felt he must be receiving the ultimate proof of Dr. Reginald Brown's proposition that, when she received proper training and management, a woman's pleasure would flow naturally from the masterful pleasure of the man to whom she belonged. When, at the point of spending himself, he withdrew from his girl's mouth and told her to lie on her back with her legs raised, Amanda obeyed immediately, her eyes darting up to his for only a moment as if to confirm that, indeed, James Coventry meant now to have his way and to deflower her according to his natural right.

He felt no need to speak further, or instruct Amanda more fully just now. The time for fucking, for his manly pleasure, had come, and he meant to enjoy himself. He put the head of his cock inside the entrance of his young lady's cunt, and merely enjoyed the sensation of being there, inside her, for a moment as she sighed, becoming used to the feeling.

Holding his stiff length in his left hand and kneeling so that he could look down at the first fucking of Miss Amanda Eaker, James moved the head up and down, in and out, watching the lascivious sight of a hard penis inside a vagina bared for the greater pleasure of its owner. He pushed in until Amanda gave a little cry of pain, his eyes greedily drinking in the scene: himself above and his naked girl below, about to become a woman under his cock.

Her eyes had closed, and she had caught her lower lip between her teeth. She held her knees up and apart as James had told her to do, making the sweetest, lewdest vision he had ever beheld. Still moving his cock gently, so as to draw little whimpers from her, he took a final moment to admire her youthful beauty, and a tenderness filled his heart that made him want to claim her in every way—erotic, yes, but also in those softer ways that filled the novels: flowers and walks across verdant meadows.

But the natural need was upon him, urgently, and though he would certainly walk over many meadows with the girl whose maiden flower he would now pluck, the time for the soft pleasures of the spring lay in the future. Now, he meant to fuck.

James gripped Amanda's thighs firmly in his hands. He looked down at the joining of his body to hers, and then he thrust hard through her maidenhead, with a little grunt of pleasure at the exquisite tightness of her cunt. Amanda cried out, but James began without delay to fuck in earnest, encouraged by Dr. Brown's thoughts on the matter, in his essay.

A girl's defloration under the penis of a natural man should be a time of service for her. O natural man, you must now stop your ears to her cries, no matter how heart-rending they may be. Your girl must learn, the first time your manhood moves in her vagina, that a part she thought her own will belong to her master henceforth.

Soon, when you take your pleasure along that path between her thighs, shaped for your penis by the providence of heaven, she too will feel the pleasure heaven has awarded to woman in order that she be encouraged to allow a natural man his rights. At first coitus, however, though she will usually feel some of that pleasure already, it will be mingled with the pain of her defloration, as your bloodstained penis moves vigorously inside her until you find your release and she receives your seed for the first time where it may quicken and make her not just woman, but mother of your strong children also.

Use this first occasion of coitus, then, to teach your girl without words that her vagina is principally the place of your pleasure. Thrust manfully. Ride in strength. Take the stimulus provided by the proud sight of your penis moving swiftly in and out of her vagina. If she squirms, hold her fast until you have finished your ride and given her the proof of your pleasure.

Every true man will feel some guilt in deflowering his beloved and seeing the proof, in her maiden blood, of the great change he has wrought between her legs. That hurt will soon be soothed, and what will remain in the new-made woman will be her memory of how well, and how thoroughly, you mastered her.

The sweetness of the sensation of being inside Amanda's adorable cunt, its velvet tightness that seemed perfectly fitted to James' cock just as Dr. Brown maintained it to have been, by heaven, enraptured him so thoroughly that he knew he would spend very soon. He did watch his bloodstained manhood moving back and forth, and that made the pleasure even greater: to know this cunt belonged to him now, and that he might fuck it any time he wished, seemed to make the seed boil in his balls.

Amanda's cries rose higher, and though he did feel the pang of guilt to which the doctor referred, those cries also aroused him even more as his hips flashed back and forth, seeking more and more of the pleasure her little cunt gave to his cock. He looked into her face again, and as if she could sense his gaze, she opened her eyes. The submissive look there, the way her furrowed brow spoke of pain that she welcomed because he gave it to her, drove him into his climax, and he grunted loud as the seed came. He held himself deeply inside her, his hands firmly around her waist, while his cock pulsed and the ecstasy passed through his whole body.

"What a good girl," he said gently, looking into her eyes. Suddenly he felt the need to reward her, and he moved his right hand to the higher place, where her little clitoris lay hidden in the wonderfully complicated hood whose operation Dr. Brown had shown him that afternoon. He began to rub her there, in little circles.

Amanda's eyes went wide. "My angel," she whispered.

James smiled. "Keep these legs open, darling. You shall spend with my cock still inside your cunny."

She did, and to James' surprise he had become erect again even before his girl cried out her climax, the sweet spasms of her cunt rousing him to new strength. The result was less comfortable for Amanda then she might have wished, he reflected later, but again the need had come upon him. He turned her over and made her masturbate for him, her face in the sheet, while he fondled her bottom to remind her that she would soon have his cock inside her tiny anus.

Then, astride her, he fucked her cunt again, dog-fashion as he had promised. He lasted much longer this time, looking down to his heart's content at the way his penis went in and out, still bloodstained, so close to the little flower of her bottom-hole. The feeling of her creamy, youthful buttocks against his lap as Amanda's cries attested that James rode his girl as vigorously as even the doctor could wish drove him nearly mad with arousal, but his earlier climax ensured that he could enjoy that feeling at great length.

The room was cool, but a sheen of perspiration had covered both their bodies by the time James held her hips tightly and pumped his seed into her womb again with three little jerks, his body feeling near to disintegration, as it seemed always to do after working so hard for a climax. Under him, Amanda whimpered still with the pleasure of her busy fingers, but James felt a sudden possessiveness and drew her hand from between her legs. He pulled it gently back and laid it, the fingers glistening with her arousal, upon her back, enjoying this small exercise of his rights over his girl's body.

Amanda turned her face back over her left shoulder, a distressed look in her eyes, almost as if she feared James might whip her. In the indignant tension of her pretty upper lip, too, James thought he could read her frustration at not being allowed another climax.

Assuming a mock gravity but in reality as contented as he had ever felt in his life—indeed as he thought it possible for him to feel—James said, "No more of that, now, darling. Your little cunny has had enough for the moment."

He wished he need not dismount from her: he felt with extraordinary keenness the pleasure of what Dr. Brown called *sheer simple mastery*. To bestride, naked, his naked young lady, with his cock still ensconced though it had slackened; to hold her naughty hand behind her... the sheer possession of Amanda that way fired his blood in a fashion far beyond the erotic. He had exercised his natural rights, and he would do so again, very soon. The knowledge made him feel precisely, he thought, as the doctor predicted he would.

Once you have deflowered your young lady, natural man, she belongs to you. You must care for her, and provide for her, because she has permitted you the most precious enjoyment a man can have upon the earth. Here lies the truly natural relation: not in the thoughtless rutting of animals but in the care that only man can feel. This belonging, at the same time it confers such responsibility, also will make you feel yourself the emperor of the new, natural world that has opened between the two of you in that act of coitus.

Do not misunderstand! Your responsibility to her, and her submissive service to you, do not mean that any false standards of what the world is pleased to call 'fidelity' apply to your union with your young lady. If you take my counsel, natural man, you will lend your young lady to other natural men, and enjoy their young ladies in turn. You will perhaps invite several natural men to enjoy your young lady at once, either alongside you or while you observe for your greater pleasure. You will perhaps form a club with other natural men, so that you may enjoy your young lady alongside theirs, according to a rota agreed among you, teaching all the young ladies how to give one another pleasure as you observe and then enjoy them as you please.

All this follows from that moment when you have taken your young lady's maidenhead. As befits your natural strength and dominance, you have conquered, and your conquest will continue. As befits your natural mercy and kindness, you will cherish and provide.

James stroked the perfect bottom, the perfect hip, of his young lady, Miss Amanda Eaker. She had called him her angel, and he intended to live up to that name. The exercise of his natural rights, according to Dr. Brown's scheme, might seem to much of the world a monstrous way in which to go about an angelic ministry. James knew, though, that with the doctor's help he could find his way toward heaven—a different heaven, perhaps, than the one to which the village schoolmistress might go, let alone Mr. Charlton and Mr. Penny, if they managed to escape the other place. For James, however, and for Amanda, it seemed to him a heaven worth the aspiration.

After Sister Stone had come to help Amanda clean up, and a junior sister had changed the sheet, James returned to his young lady's cell and lay beside her all night. Twice he woke her, to have her cunt again—once as they lay on their right sides, Amanda's left knee pulled up so that James could plunge inside her as she moaned fretfully under him; then, toward morning, with Amanda kneeling and bending her face down to present her cunt as James crouched astride and fucked until he thought his legs might give out before he spent into the velvet sheath that he knew from Amanda's woeful cries must be very sore.

He held her very close after that, the counterpane at last over them. The first light of dawn crept into the high window. "I am sorry, darling," he said softly. "I know your cunny must very tender, but I could not resist."

"It is all right," Amanda whispered, though her eyes were bright with tears. "I'm glad… I'm glad you like… you know, *having* me... that way."

"Do you like fucking, darling?" he asked.

Amanda nodded, a little smile upon her lips. "I like pleasing you, just the way Dr. Brown said I would. Even though it hurts, it still feels good somehow."

CHAPTER FOURTEEN

Dr. Brown supervised Miss Eaker's first training with the other young ladies the next day. All the girls were allowed to sleep in, just as if they were fine ladies, and had their breakfast in bed, brought to them by the two junior nursing sisters, Tabitha and Dorcas. Dr. Brown congratulated Mr. Coventry as he emerged from Miss Eaker's cell after Tabitha had gone in with her tray.

"We shall move Miss Eaker to the third floor today, and you shall have her anus there tonight. Your own things have been moved into a room on that same floor, which you'll share with a Mr. Stallings, whom you'll meet at breakfast I feel certain. Neither of you will sleep there often, of course, as you'll be with Miss Eaker or another young lady most nights, but it's a place to keep your things and to dress for dinner."

Mr. Coventry nodded. "Thank you, Doctor. Amanda will be trained with the other young ladies today?"

"That's right. As I said yesterday, you may watch in the observation lounge that adjoins the main training room. Most of the gentleman do, especially when their girls are just beginning. I imagine you'll find it quite diverting."

• • • • • • •

The main training room resembled nothing so much as the sort of ballroom one found at a dancing academy, though the floor was usually covered in soft mats rather than left bare. The bareness was of course all on the part of the young ladies who received their lessons there, before the mirrors that lined the walls and turned their six lovely nubile forms into an infinity of sweet young breasts, cunts, and pert buttocks.

"Miss Eaker, these are Miss Booth, Miss Dixon, Miss Reynolds, Miss Parker, and Miss Miller," the doctor said. Miss Eaker turned red and chewed her lower lip as each naked girl came to shake her hand, whispering her *pleased to make your acquaintance*s in a barely audible voice.

"As you can see, your fellow pupils here at my college have lost most of their modesty, as you yourself soon will, Miss Eaker," he said, frowning at her to show that she must not think her blushes became her, the way she had been educated to think of them. "You had coitus several times last night, and your vagina is now fully at the disposal of Mr. Coventry and any other man to whom he chooses to furnish you. All of your schoolmates have grown accustomed to the same position: they have had the penises of several different gentlemen inside their vaginas, their mouths, and their anuses, just as you soon will. We must rid you of this modesty as soon as possible. Having Sister Stone train your anus while the rest of the girls watch is the best way to begin, I believe."

As Miss Eaker's eyes went wide, the sister, who had been waiting with her black leather bag by her, seated on a chair by the door of the training room, came forward holding the training phallus.

"Turn around and kneel down, now, miss," the iron-grey-haired woman said gruffly. "Then bend over, just as if your gentleman were going to put his penis in your vagina from behind to have coitus with you, as he did last night."

"Wh-what... what is that thing?" Miss Eaker stammered, looking at the device, six inches long and fashioned of black India rubber.

"It is a training phallus," Dr. Brown said. "Sister Stone will use it to teach you to relax the muscles of your bottom so that Mr. Coventry can penetrate your anus and have intercourse with you there when he prefers that mode of masculine enjoyment."

Miss Eaker looked wildly at the other girls, as if to ask their assistance in warding off the terrible lesson.

"Miss Booth," the doctor said, "if you please, tell Miss Eaker how Mr. Graham has specified you be trained." He turned to Miss Eaker to elaborate. "Here at my college, on behalf of those I call proven natural men, I undertake to train young ladies like Miss Booth after their deflorations. When I am satisfied with her training I will send her to Mr. Graham for keeping in a little cottage in the park of his country house." He turned back to the girl in question, to find her blushing slightly. "Now, now, Miss Booth. Have I not just finished telling Miss Eaker that you other young ladies have lost your modesty?"

"I'm sorry, Doctor," the lovely Miss Booth said, unconsciously putting her right hand behind herself as if to ward off punishment for the blush and perhaps also at the memory of her special anal training.

"No harm done," the doctor assured her. "I'm certain Miss Eaker finds your blush rather reassuring. Remember what I always tell you, girls: obey without hesitation, and your bottoms need never feel the strap or the cane in anger. Your blushes are no more under your control than the natural vaginal lubrication that your bodies exude when it is time for a man to exercise his natural rights and to take his pleasure inside you. I shall never punish you for such involuntary things, nor will any natural man. But please proceed, and tell your new schoolmate about your special training."

Miss Booth frowned and bit her lip. For a moment Dr.

Brown thought the girl might need a spanking from Sister Stone to get started, as she had the last time she had been told to masturbate. Then she began her little tale, however, and the doctor could see that her training had gone to good effect, despite the lingering modesty. Mr. Graham would, he thought, be pleased if he could see his young lady now; Dr. Brown would write to him later today to inform him of Miss Booth's progress.

"You see, my master Mr. Graham has heard of a custom in foreign lands, though perhaps he truly only made that up like a fairy story," the little auburn-haired girl said confidingly, in a tone that signified both her acceptance of her gentleman's protection and her anxiety about the extent of his appetites where her submission was concerned. "He says it is called the way of the bottom girl."

Miss Eaker's eyes went wide in apparent alarm. "What does it mean?" she whispered.

Miss Booth shot a nervous glance at Sister Stone, undoubtedly because that worthy nurse had taken on the majority of the rigorous training regimen Dr. Brown had devised to meet Mr. Graham's requirements.

Her voice fell to a murmur, scarcely audible. "It means that I am to serve him and his guests... you see, there is a special..." Her face had gone bright pink now, and Dr. Brown did not blame her for it though he aimed eventually to have Miss Booth able to speak straightforwardly and without shame about even the lewd requirements of her life with Mr. Graham. The fabulous *Way of the Bottom Girl* invented by Mr. Graham and told to Miss Booth as a sort of Arabian Nights romance stirred Dr. Brown's blood, too, but the girl would certainly need several months of training before she could speak of it without embarrassment, despite having already given the doctor clear signs of pleasure in the extremely vigorous anal coitus to which her master wished to dedicate her body.

"Well," she continued. "Mr. Graham calls it an *arse saddle*, and I must be strapped into it with my bottom up and my face covered, and then all the gentlemen Mr. Graham has invited will…" Miss Booth's words trailed off as she cast her eyes to the floor.

"Go on, dear," said Sister Stone, who tended to develop a real affection for the girls she must train to the more rigorous sorts of sexual service. "You're doing fine."

Miss Eaker's eyes had only grown larger and rounder, and her own face blazed as red as a sunset.

"They'll take turns," Miss Booth managed to whisper. "You know, in my bottom. They won't be allowed to put their penises in my vagina at all, he says, because he wants to keep my vagina for himself." Having finished this terrible narrative, she raised her eyes and Dr. Brown watched Amanda Eaker's brow furrow to see that Miss Booth had a little smile on her mouth. "So the sisters use the training phallus on me every day for a long time, in the arse saddle, to get my bottom ready. There is to be a party, a fortnight hence, when Mr. Graham will offer my anus for the first time."

Miss Eaker turned desperately to Dr. Brown. "James— that is to say, Mr. Coventry… He won't… not like that, will he?"

Dr. Brown sighed. "Miss Eaker, I had hoped that Miss Booth's tale would demonstrate to you that my natural men's requirements include acts of coitus for which a girl like you must be well prepared. Soon, you will be able to express your gratitude for the way the training phallus has taught you to open as your gentleman deserves. But I am afraid that your reluctance to obey and to receive your training shows a need for discipline."

"Shall I fetch the cane, Doctor?" asked Sister Stone.

Miss Eaker whirled to look at her in horror. "Please… I'll…" She knelt on the floor and began to bend over.

"That is not sufficient now, Miss Eaker," said Dr. Brown. "Yes, sister, the cane if you please. Just six, I think. Miss Dixon and Miss Parker, please bring the whipping block. You two will hold Miss Eaker down while I cane her.

Then she will receive her training right there, in order to relate the ideas of punishment and anal coitus in her mind and heart."

Amanda Eaker's little bottom soon rose over the block, a modified version of the boys' public school article that presented a girl's backside more prominently as she knelt upon the step, clutching the block's well-worn far corners. The device had straps to secure the miscreant for punishment, but when other girls were present Dr. Brown preferred to have them do the office of keeping the girl to be flogged in place until her bottom bore the signs of his justice to the extent he had decided.

Miss Eaker wailed as Thea Dixon and Cressida Parker led her to the block and helped her bend over it. "Please, Doctor! Not the cane! I am sure that Mr. Coventry—I am sure that my master does not..."

"Oh, he wishes it," Dr. Brown assured the girl, thinking of the men watching from the comfortable observation lounge. "Your gentleman has brought you here because he understands your need for discipline. With six stripes across your pretty rear end, you will not hesitate again to obey, for a good long time."

She sobbed as he made his practice cuts through the air with the half-inch rattan the sister brought him. Then she screamed as he caned her, as if her heart would break, pleading for mercy and calling for her *James* to rescue her. Though Dr. Brown did not usually give many strokes of the cane, he always pulled his arm back at full length, and the welts he laid across a young lady's posterior always lasted several days. None of the other girls had dry eyes, either, as young Miss Eaker struggled against Miss Dixon's and Miss Parker's restraining hands, her lovely young bottom clenching and unclenching in the agony of her just reward.

Sister Stone stepped forward with the training phallus and the lubricating oil, then, and Miss Eaker cried out anew as the older woman began to work her anus with rigor.

"Hush, child," said the nurse. "Relax, and open this little

ring. You can do it. You know you can. Push out, just as you know how. There. That's it."

The girl gave a great sob as she felt herself held open by the nurse's terrible implement. The other girls watched with some alarm as the black India rubber disappeared into their new schoolmate's rump.

"Now a few minutes of simulated coitus," Dr. Brown said with satisfaction. Sister Stone began to move the phallus in and out of Miss Eaker's anus, as Mr. Coventry would do that evening. Miss Eaker gave only forlorn little whimpers now, as she learned her difficult lesson.

"Any questions, girls?" the doctor asked as the little show of the new girl's discipline over the block continued.

Miss Miller raised her hand. "Will Miss Eaker wear a plug in her anus, Doctor?" Beatrix Miller herself, like Thea Dixon, had frequently to wear an anal widener. Girls who wore them, Dr. Brown observed, tended to form a little sorority inside the college.

"That will be up to Mr. Coventry, after he has enjoyed her there with his penis, Miss Miller."

Miss Eaker gave another little sob at that, and Miss Miller seemed satisfied.

Miss Booth raised her hand. "What will we be doing after Miss Eaker's bottom training, doctor?"

"I'm glad you asked, Miss Booth," the doctor said, smiling. "We have a visitor today, from the colonies." He took his bell from his pocket and rang it. A large man with very dark skin stepped through the door from the observation lounge.

"Girls, I should like to present to you Mr. Chelimo."

"Hello, young ladies," said the cultured colonial, whose refined words matched neither the nudity of his person nor the enormity of the erect penis he pumped gently in his right hand.

Sister Stone finished with Amanda Eaker's anus, then, so she too could behold the man who strode confidently toward the naked girls.

"Today," said Dr. Brown, "you girls will learn to please a natural man from a foreign land, whose penis will test your erotic training very severely."

CHAPTER FIFTEEN

Amanda's only role in the fucking of her new schoolmates by Mr. Chelimo was, thank heaven, to observe. Even to watch, though, herself naked and with her bottom-hole feeling so strange and itchy after the terrible training of Sister Stone's mock penis, seemed to change her—train her in a different way.

Dr. Brown had her stand against the wall with her hands upon her head. "Don't think of covering your eyes, Miss Eaker, or turning away. You must take note, and learn, so that next time, if your master permits it, the training by a sizable penis of your mouth, vagina, and anus can proceed smoothly."

So Amanda saw the fear in the other girls' eyes as they had to kneel in front of Mr. Chelimo, and she saw the way he held their heads tightly as he used their mouths, one after the other. The sight of the foamy stuff that must be made of the girls' spittle and Mr. Chelimo's sexual liquor gracing the lips of Miss Dixon and Miss Booth, Miss Reynolds and Miss Miller and Miss Parker, as the long, dark cock went ceaselessly in and out, made her feel faint.

But the way they cried out when he fucked their bottoms nearly made her swoon dead away, so that Sister Stone led her to her own chair to keep Amanda from falling and hurting herself.

"You just put your head down between your knees if you feel that way," said the woman who had worked Amanda's anus so rigorously that now, as she sat, her bottom didn't even feel like it belonged to her any longer. "You're white as a sheet, child—as well you may be. I've submitted to some men like Mr. Chelimo in my day, and enjoyed it, but I know how it scares a girl to see it."

In the center of the room the other young ladies of the college knelt in a line and reached back to spread their bottom-cheeks, as Mr. Chelimo went from offered rump to offered rump. The rigor with which he possessed those little flowers, filling them again and again with his enormous manhood, sent wails of discomfort to the rafters.

Amanda looked curiously at the nursing sister. It hadn't occurred to her that Sister Stone must have had some of the same strange training the young ladies of Dr. Brown's college received, but she supposed the truth couldn't be otherwise. If the statuesque middle-aged woman had submitted to a natural man as her master, in her day, it seemed hard to tell now, as Sister Stone gave a reassuring smile.

Not for the first time, Amanda wondered whether this would all seem different to her if she were married. She felt a sudden desperation to know whether the other girls' gentlemen had promised to marry them, though she felt sure the answer must be negative in every case. James' words, *I may very well marry you*, uttered themselves in her heart, and then she heard again the way he called her a *good girl* when she spent for him, under his naughty fingers or under his pounding cock.

The young ladies being fucked by Mr. Chelimo's enormous cock must be undergoing that ordeal because their gentlemen said they should—that this dark-skinned man might come and fuck the girls who belonged to those natural men. Natural men like James Coventry, it seemed, who had brought their young ladies here to Dr. Brown's college to make their cunnies and bottoms more pleasurable.

The warm feeling began again between Amanda's thighs at that thought, and suddenly she wanted her bottom to please James, whether or not he promised to marry her. She wanted it because in that moment she saw in the shameful way Mr. Chelimo fucked the young ladies' bottoms what Dr. Brown meant when he talked about natural rights. Amanda, too, had the right to be fucked that way: the right to leave behind the world of the squire of Renford-on-Tees and of Mr. Charlton. Amanda had the right to enjoy her angel's possession of her, without worrying what society would think.

• • • • • • •

It seemed the doctor had appointed to dinner the very old-fashioned hour of two o'clock. The meal seemed at first a strange affair, with clothed gentlemen and naked girls, but the conversation struck Amanda as convivial, and to her surprise not an openly salacious word passed any gentleman's lips.

Though it seemed that fucking was not referred to at the table, discipline apparently might be. Mr. Stallings, seated to her left, asked her whether Mr. Coventry preferred to use the cane, the strap, or the birch upon her. Blushing, Amanda confessed that she didn't know yet, for her gentleman had not yet punished her himself with anything but his hand.

"Coventry, is that true?" Mr. Stallings called across the table to where James had engaged Miss Parker in conversation. "Have you not flogged your girl yet? Bless me! I thrashed Beatrix before I did anything else." He turned to Amanda again. "She was a parlor maid in my cousin's house, and I caught her looking through my things. As soon as I birched her, I knew I had to bring her to Dr. Brown's."

"That's right," James said forthrightly, giving Amanda

one of the little smiles that made her heart beat faster. "A brute of a farmer whipped her soundly, I'm afraid, before I could carry her off to safety."

"Quite right," said Dr. Brown from the head of the table. "Mr. Stallings, you should take a lesson from Mr. Coventry, more advanced in this study though you may be."

The doctor cast his eye on Miss Miller, who had turned her rosy face down to address her potatoes. Amanda felt a surge of affection for the little flaxen-haired girl, who had seemed to have had the hardest time of all the young ladies with Mr. Chelimo's enormous penis, crying out that she couldn't take the whole length of it in her tender cunny, as the other girls had held her legs open for him to plunge inside her as he liked. Now at dinner, though, she seemed very bright-eyed, and Amanda thought she even saw a smile play upon her lips at having her justly birched bottom discussed.

"Miss Eaker's bottom," the doctor continued, "was in such a state that further discipline was inadvisable. Granted that Miss Miller's frequent birchings have produced good results..." Did Amanda see the smile again? "...but in my experience a bit of sparing the rod does not spoil the girl— so long as the rod be consistently and firmly applied nonetheless, as Miss Eaker found out to her sorrow this morning. I imagine her seat isn't a very comfortable one just now. Is it, Miss Eaker?"

He turned his gaze to Amanda, and it was her turn to blush. She had grown so interested in the table talk that she had nearly forgotten about the stinging soreness of the cane, and the way she had screamed over the block.

"No, Doctor," she said softly.

"Doctor?" James said. "May I ask a question concerning modesty?"

"Certainly, Mr. Coventry—especially as I am quite sure it will be a very good one."

"My Amanda has just blushed at your words respecting the flogging you were forced to give her."

Now, as Miss Miller had fixed her eyes on her potatoes, Amanda must do the same, her face burning still more.

"You have said that we must do our best to drive the blushes out of our young ladies, have you not?"

Dr. Brown smiled and nodded. "I see. Yes, that is a matter I will take up in the second edition of my essay, and you're quite perceptive to enquire about it, Mr. Coventry. Mr. Shaw, would you care to hazard a guess as to what I plan to write on the subject?" The doctor addressed the whole of the long table, then, everyone having fallen silent at the exchange among him, Mr. Stallings, and James concerning Miss Miller and Amanda herself. "You all have seen, I think, perhaps even including our new arrivals, that Miss Reynolds, Mr. Shaw's young lady, has nearly lost her modesty when it comes, for example, to displaying her vagina or her anus and offering them to a strange man like Mr. Chelimo. She will still blush, however, when this immodesty is referred to here at dinner, or—as Miss Eaker just has done—if Mr. Shaw should make reference to some naughtiness for which he has had to spank her over his knee."

Sure enough, Stella Reynolds' face had gone quite pink.

"I imagine," Mr. Shaw said thoughtfully, "that you will write something in the nature of what I believe you said to me last week: that Stella's blushes in the bedroom, or the training room, and respecting my natural rights—for example to loan her vagina and anus to Mr. Chelimo or any other natural man—differ from the blushes of the drawing room."

"Precisely," said the doctor, nodding and turning to James. "I was perhaps too general in my words in the first edition. If we were to drive away *all* these young ladies' blushes, you gentlemen might not take them out in a society still composed of more unnatural men and women than natural ones. Our task is to make them shameless in your arms and in the arms of the other men to whom you offer them, rather than to make them *altogether* shameless and thus unfit for company."

• • • • • • •

After dinner, the young ladies, instead of going up to the drawing room as might happen in an ordinary house, went to their cells.

"You must get upon your bed on your hands and knees," Miss Dixon said softly to Amanda as the girls dispersed in the third floor corridor, "with your bottom to the door."

"Why?" Amanda asked, mystified.

"It's time for our enemas." Then, as if she saw the startled expression on Amanda's face, she said, "Don't worry—if you do as the sister says, it feels nice."

She disappeared into her own cell, leaving Amanda to scamper into hers, for she had heard the voice of Sister Stone talking to her junior nursing sisters, and the rattle, she thought, of some kind of trolley.

"All right, miss," said Sister Dorcas as she entered Amanda's cell. "It's time to get your anus nice and clean for your gentleman. I know it's your first time, but don't make a fuss and it will be over in a wink. You're a good girl to get on your bed like that, all ready for it."

Amanda turned her face back over her shoulder and watched the woman of thirty or so approach, holding in one hand a sort of can with a length of tubing wrapped around it. In her other hand she had a jar of some jelly that Amanda supposed must be the same as had been on the doctor's speculum and the horrid phallus trainer.

"Now you had the trainer up your bum this morning— is that right, miss?"

"Y-yes," Amanda stammered.

"This will be much nicer than that was," the nurse reassured her. "I'm just going to get you ready, now, with my finger, so the nozzle goes in comfortable-like."

Sister Dorcas' finger made Amanda give a little whimper as it moved gently in and out. "There, miss, that's not so bad, is it? You're going to have to have a big penis in there later, aren't you? So there's no need to fuss about my finger, is there?"

No, there was no need. The slick finger actually made Amanda's face get hot because it felt so nice. The warmth began anew between her thighs, in the bare cunny she knew the nurse could see so clearly, under the place where she now inserted something cool and narrow.

"Now I'll let the soapy water flow in," Sister Dorcas said. "Once I'm done, you'll sit on the pot for me, and then you'll be all ready for your gentleman."

Amanda's brow furrowed at the delicious, shameful feeling, and at the thought of sitting on the pot in front of the nurse. From down the corridor, a cry of discomfort arose that made her heart beat fast.

"What's that?" she asked fearfully.

"Oh," Sister Dorcas said. "Miss Parker has to have a punishment enema today. She answered back to Sister Stone this morning. She'll have a whole quart up her bum, and keep it there for ten minutes. Then after she lets it out, sister will spank her." She pulled the nozzle from Amanda's bottom. "All right, miss. I'll get the pot. Get up and come over like a good girl. We'll get you nice and fresh for the penis to go in just as it should in a pretty young lady like yourself."

CHAPTER SIXTEEN

Before James went to Amanda's cell to fuck her bottom, Dr. Brown invited his newest cocksman into his study, and spoke with him at some length.

"As you know, Mr. Coventry, I have no expectations with regard to the social station you intend your young lady to occupy."

James nodded, uncertain in what direction the doctor intended the conversation to proceed.

"Girls who have matriculated from the College of Advanced Study have gone on to become duchesses on the one hand and harlots on the other. You, Mr. Coventry, would not be here if I were not sure you understand the fundamental tenet of my philosophy concerning social relations."

Still rather mystified, James shifted in the Chesterfield chair across the neatly kept desk from the doctor, and said, "That when a natural man exercises his erotic rights with a girl, any station in which he places her will follow in due order, you mean?"

Dr. Brown nodded. "I bring the matter up with you now because I regard the moment in Miss Eaker's training at which you now stand—this period just before you have anal coitus with her for the first time—as an extremely important one. I have employed with some success this gesture of consulting with the gentleman who is to take the virginity of his young lady's backside in previous cases. Thus my discourse with you this evening. It will be of great use to you and Miss Eaker to make some resolution now concerning her future."

James felt his eyes narrow as he shifted again in the chair. He opened his mouth to say that he thought he had made it clear that his financial means were still subject to some uncertainty—though since arriving in Westmoreland he had in fact had some very encouraging correspondence—but Dr. Brown continued in a reassuring tone before James could utter a syllable.

"Do not misunderstand me, please, Mr. Coventry. I am not playing the aggrieved father with you, demanding to know how you will provide for your young lady! We both know how unsuitable that would be!"

The doctor chuckled, and James joined in the mirth. "Then...?" he asked, tilting his head quizzically to the side. The ornate old longcase clock in the corner tocked a few seconds away. The anticipation of the lascivious act to come, in Amanda's cell, made his palms itch.

The doctor chuckled again. "I know how impatient you are to enjoy Miss Eaker's bottom. That is in part why I use this occasion to attempt to settle things: not only is the gentleman's mind—your mind—focused on the extremity of the enjoyment you will take in the exercise of this very special natural right, the one that you know I consider to be the supreme right, but of course the girl's mind is similarly focused. Whether you discuss these matters with Miss Eaker tonight, before or after you master her anus, or not, your actions in her cell—that is to say, the *way* you go about subjecting her anus to your enjoyment—will inevitably speak to her in their own fashion, and begin to prepare her for her future life, whatever it may be."

James nodded, finally understanding, though of course

the doctor's words had caused a new swelling of his cock that made him eager to bring the conversation to a close.

"I think I follow you now, Doctor," he said. "Let me say that I haven't yet made my decision as to whether Miss Eaker will be a suitable wife..."

"You are considering marrying her, though?" the doctor asked. "From what I hear of your prospects, you could marry a wealthy wife and keep Miss Eaker comfortably in the country."

James felt his face darken, and the doctor clearly noticed the change of expression.

"Forgive me for stating the matter so baldly, Mr. Coventry. To proceed from my earlier premise, a gentleman who plans to marry a young lady has anal coitus with her in one way, while a gentleman who plans to keep her, or even to make her comfortable while leaving her to other men— what some would call *putting her away*—penetrates that special orifice in a different manner. Do you still follow me?"

James did, but he didn't very much like where the path seemed to lead.

"That isn't to say," the doctor continued inexorably, "that a prospective husband should not subject his future bride to anal coitus of the same rigorous kind he might have with a trollop whose bottom he has no compunction about leaving in an uncomfortable state. Many a wife of a natural man feels the same tenderness in the morning that the trollop does. It is my considered opinion, however, that in this supreme exercise of natural masculine rights, when a man teaches his young lady that every part of her person was fashioned for his pleasure, and that she may deny him none of it, the subtlest of messages whether in word or bodily gesture has great import."

James nodded, a little grimly.

"And of course," Dr. Brown said now with an orotund air that seemed to indicate that he intended to bring the chief head of his discourse to an end, "even if I am incorrect in that opinion, to possess a girl's anus represents a sort of erotic act and a sort of claiming of what the world considers her modesty so complete and irrevocable that even men such as you and I, who reject the world's conventions, should take some thought for the girl's fate."

He had not seen it thus before, James realized, and his gratitude to the doctor returned. For a moment, as the clock chimed softly the hour of six—the hour appointed for Miss Amanda Eaker's anal defloration—he searched his heart as he gazed into the Scotsman's twinkling blue eyes. Then, at first to his surprise and then quickly to his confident joy, he realized that he had the answer—that he had had it inside him from the moment he found Amanda in the little grove.

He wanted a pretty girl's anus to fuck whenever he pleased—with the help of Dr. Brown's essay, college, and words of wisdom, James knew he must not deny that essential fact of his dominant masculinity. He also, however, loved Miss Amanda Eaker for the whole of her: her good, loving heart and her curious mind as well as the beauty that made his own heart ache even while it made his cock grow hard in anticipation of possessing her and mastering her sexually.

"I shall marry her, Doctor," he said. "Whatever our prospects, we shall marry."

• • • • • • •

In Amanda's cell, all was prepared. She awaited him with punished bottom up and blushing face down, the presentation to his eye of those pert eighteen-year-old bottom-cheeks making him think of the 'arse saddle' Miss Booth had told Amanda about in the training room, as James and Henry Stallings watched from the observation lounge. He didn't think he would like to offer Amanda's bottom to guests the way it seemed Wilson Graham—a school friend of James' as it happened—would. He thought, however, that he wouldn't mind putting his young lady—

his bride—in an arse saddle for his own private enjoyment, and he wondered if Wilson would share the design of the article with him.

James untied the belt of his dressing gown and took his cock in his left hand, the better to enjoy the sight of his young lady naked over the leather-covered bolster the nursing sisters had, it seemed, placed under her hips to raise her creamy bottom, accented so nicely by its morning flogging, for his enjoyment. How else, he wondered, had they prepared Amanda? He felt a little surprised that she had not turned her face to look at him.

"Darling, did they tell you not to turn around?" he asked curiously.

"Yes, sir," Amanda said softly into the covers, her voice muffled. "And I'm not to speak unless spoken to, so..." Her quavery voice trailed off, then began again even more uncertainly. "So I don't interfere with your pleasure. And I must tell you that if you want to have me strapped down to the bed, you may summon Sister Dorcas to do it."

James smiled broadly. "How else did they prepare you, darling?" He advanced a few steps, so that he could lay his left hand on the little bottom with its six red cane marks. Amanda gave a tiny whimper as he began to stroke her gently there, adoring the tautness and roundness of the pert cheeks under his caressing fingers.

"Th-they cleaned me... there... with an enema, s-so I won't get you dirty, Sister Dorcas said. And they... they oiled me, too, with that same jelly. Sister Stone made me practice opening, with her fingers."

"I'm very glad to hear it," James said gently, still pumping his cock in his left hand and fondling Amanda's bottom with his right. "I think you must already understand very well how important bottom sex is to me, and the other gentlemen here."

"Yes, sir," Amanda whispered. "Will they...? Will they, also...?"

"Fuck your bottom? Yes, they will. That's part of your

course of study here at Dr. Brown's college."

Amanda swallowed hard.

"And Mr.... Mr. Chelimo?"

James watched her little hands clench into fists, as if at the thought of that abandoned scene in the training room that he and Stallings had watched with such interest.

"I understand that Mr. Chelimo comes here once a fortnight or so, darling," he said. "On his next visit, he will fuck you just as he fucks the other girls."

Amanda made no reply, but James heard her breathing grow quicker, puffing in and out of her nostrils. The thought of the long, dark cock going in and out of Amanda's cunt as she cried out upon the enormity of it made him pump his own cock harder, and he felt he couldn't keep himself from his supreme right any longer. He climbed upon the bed and said, "Reach back and open your bottom, Amanda. Prepare yourself to submit to me."

She obeyed, and James spent a long moment just enjoying the sight of her spread bottom-cheeks with the sweet pink flower of her anus above the delicious pout of her cunt peeping out between her thighs. Her delicate little fingers held the punished cheeks apart, at his command, and the tiny winking eye into which he would now thrust did indeed glisten with the lubricant applied by Sister Stone's knowing fingers. Miss Amanda Eaker was ready for bottom fucking, and the good fortune fell to James Coventry, Esq. to exercise his natural right to claim this lovely young lady in her most private place. He shrugged the dressing gown from his shoulders and let it fall to the floor.

Amanda made a tiny sound in her throat as James laid the head of his cock against the narrow portal. Her bottom squirmed, and James thought of commanding her to hold it still, or even of calling the nursing sister to provide the promised service of securing his girl to her bed so that he could enter her bottom at his ease and enjoy himself there in peace.

But his conversation with Dr. Brown came to mind, and

he suddenly understood the reason for it much better than he had even after the doctor had elucidated his philosophy in such sage, persuasive words. James climbed quickly off the bed and came to stoop next to Amanda's face. Surprise was in her eyes, and for a moment he thought she would try to turn away, as if in fear of being whipped for looking him in the face.

James kissed her, long and deeply, savoring the sweet taste in her mouth that he thought must be the honey she had put in her tea. "Amanda," he asked, "will you be my wife?"

She started at that, and a shiver went through her whole body.

"I know this is an exceedingly odd way to propose," he murmured, "as least as far as the world is concerned, but I think it is the proper way, for such as I—and perhaps for such as you."

"Yes," Amanda whispered. "Yes, I... Yes, for such as I, and yes, I will be your wife, James. And..."

James kissed her again. "And what, darling?"

Amanda bit her lip and her cheeks turned pink. "Please, sir. Would you have Sister Dorcas strap me down to the bed?"

CHAPTER SEVENTEEN

Dr. Brown looked through the peephole of Miss Eaker's cell with great satisfaction. Between Mr. Coventry's muscular legs, as the cocksman flexed his knees to thrust his penis rhythmically inside Miss Eaker's pretty pink anus, he had a clear view of the erotic sight he personally found most arousing of all: a girl's well-behaved bottom—well-behaved in Miss Eaker's case because of the stout straps about her waist and upper thighs. Her hands, cuffed to the belt by which Sister Dorcas had secured her hips and backside in place, still obediently held open her punished bottom-cheeks for her gentleman's use, showing to Dr. Brown both the motions of the penis inside her and the pout of her shaved labia.

She whimpered her submission as Mr. Coventry rode in and out of her bottom at a brisk pace, murmuring words of encouragement that Dr. Brown couldn't make out entirely. The cadence, however, suggested that he employed *good girl* and *sweet bottom* with some frequency. Mr. Coventry's penis caused his young lady a good deal of discomfort, the doctor could tell from her cries, but he also could observe the vagina's clear signs of arousal as the girl underwent her first coitus in the tighter passage just above it.

116

He had not expected the cocksman to interrupt his first possession to go speak intimately with his young lady, but when the Dr. Brown saw it, he knew that Mr. Coventry had proposed. Nor was he much surprised by the request that Miss Eaker be bound to her bed for her anal session with her new fiancé: the girl clearly recognized her need to submit completely.

The doctor had no doubt that Mr. Coventry would in future be able to require anal intercourse of his young lady without binding her. Indeed, it seemed clear that he could have had her without the straps this evening, her bottom still reasonably well-behaved for its coitus. For Miss Eaker herself to acknowledge a desire to please her gentleman with the stilling of her backside he would ride, though, demonstrated a self-awareness the doctor found both striking and satisfactory.

Mr. Coventry increased his pace, the springs of the bed groaning a little in time with Miss Eaker's cries of discomfort at the depth of her gentleman's intercourse. The man stood on the brink of orgasm, the doctor could see: his young lady would be sore in the morning, and perhaps the doctor would have to advise Mr. Coventry to refrain from renewing her anal training immediately, but rigorous bottom sex had an important place in a young woman's life at the College of Advanced Study.

Though Miss Eaker had received the penis gently for the first few minutes, it was just as well she should receive it with authority now, until it ejaculated inside her bottom. Here at the end of her first session of Mr. Coventry's exercise of his supreme right over her person, it would give her the memorable lesson of his desire to possess her as deeply as he could.

A husky warning came from the gentleman, informing his young lady that she must prepare herself to receive his seed. Mr. Coventry took hold of Miss Eaker's wrists and used the traction to drive his penis into her bottom at full length, crying out himself as if thunderstruck by the force of his climax.

Dr. Brown stayed long enough at the peephole to see Mr. Coventry loose his girl from her bonds and gather her in his arms, and even to hear her giggle when her gentleman told her to lie back and hold her legs open so he might reward her for giving him so much pleasure. He closed the peephole on the sight of a fine young man tasting the heady flavor of a young vagina for the first time, while Miss Eaker's cries assumed quite a different note.

Back in his study, the doctor recorded the event in the file for Case 35.

First anal coitus 17 April 1875: very satisfactory. The gentleman has a tendency to use the anus deeply; anal training to resume in two days. In the meantime use of the vagina will be advised, as much as he pleases. The young lady requested binding to the bed: indicates that much modesty will need to be overcome, but that she is strikingly self-aware, and ready to participate in its overcoming.

Future treatment therefore indicated: the gentleman to be advised to loan the mouth and vagina tomorrow, in a side-by-side session. Use of the double masturbation saddle beforehand also to be recommended.

• • • • • • •

After dinner the next day, Dr. Brown summoned Mr. Coventry and Miss Eaker to his study, having previously confirmed with Mr. Stallings that he and Miss Miller would be happy to participate in the new couple's first side-by-side session. Mr. Stallings also declared that he saw no objection to putting Miss Miller on the masturbation saddle with Miss Eaker.

"Congratulations, Miss Eaker," the doctor began once the couple had assumed their seats across his desk from him. The piquancy of a naked young lady in his well-appointed study never failed to inspire him in his work. "You did very well last night. I'm sure Mr. Coventry has expressed his satisfaction with your anus, but I wanted to extend an expression of my own pleasure—from a medical standpoint—in what I observed when you had the penis in your bottom. I hear you two are to be married, as well, and I think Mr. Coventry has made a very fine choice of bride: a girl whose pretty mouth, vagina, and anus will give his penis great enjoyment for many years."

Miss Eaker had of course turned bright red, and though her lips parted she did not speak. Mr. Coventry reached out his hand and took hers in it.

"I've told her she must try to give up these blushes, Doctor," he said apologetically.

"That's perfectly all right, Mr. Coventry. I believe that Miss Eaker's request to be strapped down while you penetrated her anus indicates to me that she understands, and will work hard to please you. Isn't that right, Miss Eaker?"

"Yes, Doctor," the sweet girl whispered, her head bowed so that she looked only at her naked lap.

"As you know," the doctor continued, "Mr. Shaw and Miss Reynolds left this morning for America. I mention it because as the days go by you will start to notice the goings and comings here my college more and more. All that is really only to bring up the matter of the length of your own stay. Mr. Coventry intimated to me when he first wrote that he thought your stay here might have to be lengthy, Miss Eaker, but I gather from a letter I had this morning from London that he may have news concerning his prospects that he may like to share."

Mr. Coventry smiled and turned to his young lady, whose face wore the charming, inquisitive aspect of one who has heard she is to receive good news, but remains ignorant of its nature.

"That's right—very right indeed, darling. The Duke of Panton has come up trumps for me—for us, now. Apparently when he heard that you and I had come here to Dr. Brown's, he decided that I deserve his full confidence. I'm to assume management of his entire estate, and we shall go to live there, in Sussex—when we are not in town, that is."

Miss Eaker's eyes went very wide. "The Duke of Panton! But is he not very wicked?"

Dr. Brown chuckled. "Well, Miss Eaker, I must confess that I fear *you*, and Mr. Coventry, and I—and everyone here—are very wicked by the standards of the world that judges the good duke so. The duke, of the great line of Lourcy Earls of Mercester and Dukes of Panton, is the heir to a noble tradition of men exercising their natural rights. His school for young ladies, on the grounds of Panton Castle, is a sort of model of the benefits to be had by frankness in these matters—he and his mistress Miss Clarissa Halton have reshaped many a fallen girl's life for her ultimate salvation. If there were ever a place for you to lose your blushes, it would be Panton Castle." He turned to Mr. Coventry. "And Miss Eaker is to be married from there? With the aid of the duke's schoolmistress?"

The young man nodded, his face still sunny with his extraordinary good fortune. "Precisely. And, darling..." His eyes returned to Miss Eaker's. "We shall be able to bring your parents there, if they would like. And the duke even says that he has plans to bring Lord Rider down, and have that monstrous marriage of Mr. Penny's annulled. I laid out the whole matter to him, and he has taken a great interest— as indeed I thought he might, since he interests himself in whatever Dr. Brown does."

Bright tears of happiness appeared in Miss Eaker's eyes. "Truly? And may Jane... that is to say, Mrs. Penny—she is my best friend..."

"She may come to Panton too, if she likes," Mr. Coventry said with a smile. "She shall be a bridesmaid."

That made Miss Eaker blush, of course.

"Come now," said Dr. Brown, "a natural maid is a girl without false modesty, who knows how to grant her gentleman, whether master, or husband, or a man to whom her master gives her, the exercise of his erotic rights."

"But Jane... and I, I suppose..." the girl managed to say, her lovely blue eyes darting up to the doctor's for a moment, then over to Mr. Coventry's face, then back to her lap, where she held her right hand curled in an embarrassed little fist—her left being still held firmly in her gentleman's right. "We are not pure any longer. Mr. Penny—the things he did, with his conjugal rights... I know they are the same as what James has done with me, but..."

The doctor came to her aid. "But because your friend Jane has been *married* to such a man—and allow me to say clearly that I do not think this Mr. Penny, or the man who forced his pleasure upon you under the guise of a suitor, is a true, natural man such as Mr. Coventry, or the Duke of Panton—the voices in your mind, of your mother and your schoolmistress, tell you that she should not be a bridesmaid."

Miss Eaker nodded, the shining happiness in her face having given way to confusion and renewed shame.

"I am pleased to tell you, though," Dr. Brown continued, "that in the world into which you—and it appears Jane, if she wishes—are to enter, to be a maid of any kind is a matter of what one might call..." He paused to see if she would look up, and when she did he gave her a warm smile, and held her eyes, feeling sure that she could discern in his the twinkle he meant her to see there. "...*preference*. Jane shall be your bridesmaid, and I feel quite sure you will play the blushing bride to perfection."

To the doctor's delight, a radiant smile broke out on Miss Eaker's face at this news. She looked at Mr. Coventry and said softly, "Shall you like having your conjugal rights, James?"

He chuckled and kissed her hand. "I certainly shall, darling."

"To that end," said Dr. Brown, "I should like to recommend to Mr. Coventry a session for you, Miss Eaker, with Mr. Stallings and Miss Miller, in the grand bedroom."

Miss Eaker's blush returned, then, and her smile grew a

little more uncertain, but did not fade entirely.

"I think you will find, Mr. Coventry, that introducing Miss Eaker to your rights with respect to the sharing of young ladies among friends will serve to make her ready to enter fully into the connubial bliss you have in store for her. When a true man's natural rights intersect so fully with the conjugal rights he has over his bride's young body, a girl must learn to submit to be shared, and to be observed, without the false modesty with which Miss Eaker herself knows she must part."

The young lady's smile had changed to a look of helpless arousal. "What must I do?" she whispered.

"First," said the doctor, "if Mr. Coventry accepts my recommendation, you will ride with Miss Miller upon a training saddle that features two phalluses, which you will take into your vaginas. Miss Miller will watch you as you reach climax, and you will watch her. Your gentlemen, of course, will observe the entire process, providing such encouragement as seems best to them. Then you will have coitus with Mr. Coventry, while Mr. Stallings has coitus with Miss Miller, the four of you upon the same bed. Then Mr. Coventry will share your vagina with Mr. Stallings, while Mr. Stallings shares Miss Miller's vagina with him. Finally, you will watch as Mr. Coventry and Mr. Stallings enjoy Miss Miller, and after that she will observe as the two gentlemen enjoy you."

CHAPTER EIGHTEEN

Amanda felt very faint as James led her to the grand bedroom. Her mind seemed split into two parts. One part wouldn't stop thinking about the Duke of Panton and the future that it seemed awaited her in Sussex as a wife—perhaps not a *respectable* wife, as the world judged, but one under the protection of one of the greatest peers of the realm. The other part wouldn't stop thinking about the price it appeared she must now pay for this wedded bliss, made to share James and to be shared by him.

The room, in which they found Mr. Stallings and Miss Miller waiting for them, must have once been a drawing room in the days before Dr. Brown had come to turn the stately home into his lascivious college. The rich crimson velvet on the walls, and the pier glasses and gilt ornaments in the French style spoke of elegant conversation upon soft sofas and beautiful chairs.

Those articles of furniture had, however, been replaced in such a way as to make Amanda draw back against James as he ushered her into the big room. To see the three large beds, each of them big enough for two couples to fuck side-by-side, made her feel strange enough, but the article placed upon the central bed next to which Mr. Stallings and Miss Miller stood made her heart quail.

Upon a long wooden frame, placed crosswise on the

bed, two saddles had been fixed, facing one another. The frame itself stood perhaps eighteen inches off the bed, so that Amanda could tell immediately that a girl might comfortably mount it, and then ride upon it in a jockey's crouch. In the middle of the frame rose a post, and from that post on either side emerged what must be handlebars: one set for each girl to hold while riding her saddle.

The very idea of mounting thus, opposite another naked girl, their faces only a few inches apart as they must ride like men, shamefully astride and with the saddles between their thighs, made the heat come into her face. What rose from the saddles, however, heated Amanda's cheeks to fever pitch.

Out of each saddle one of the horrid black training phalluses stood a proud six inches, tilted slightly backwards from the central post so that the imitation penis might go straight into the cunny of a crouching girl.

"A marvelous device, what?" said Henry Stallings, dressed like James in one of the cocksmen's black dressing gowns. He was a tall man—even taller than James, and of a dark, almost Mediterranean complexion. "Bad luck that we can't have Miss Eaker's arse today, though. Shaw and I liked to put our girls on it and fuck them soundly up their sweet bums while they rode. Going to miss that fellow—shame you didn't get to know him." To Amanda's horror, he looked at her. "But your backside's going to feel my cock soon, I expect, Miss Eaker—never fear, though you'll only have me in your mouth and cunt today."

Beatrix Miller, with a kind of innocent wonder in her blue eyes that made Amanda remember what Dr. Brown had said about maidenhood being a matter of *preference*, looked at James. "Will you have my bottom, Mr. Coventry? Miss Eaker's cries last night made me think I might want Henry to share it with you, and now Henry says the doctor has recommended that you fuck me while he fucks Miss Eaker, but he says it's up to you whether you want to enjoy my bottom or only my cunny."

"Show Mr. Coventry your anus, my love," said Mr. Stallings. Amanda's knees felt weak as she watched Miss Miller turn around and bend over the bed, letting her long flaxen hair fall over her left shoulder as she lowered her head submissively. She put her hands back and spread her bottom-cheeks to show a little pink flower that didn't seem any less tight than Amanda imagined her own must look. Instinctively she put her hand behind her, down there, to cover her poor bottom-hole, still so sore from James' rigorous use the previous night.

The whole room seemed to whirl, as the *Panton* part of her mind and the *terrible price* part of her mind seemed to chase each other around a carousel of ideas and imagined scenes. Why did it all have to go so fast?

"You're welcome to fuck her there, of course, Coventry, even if I have to wait for my own turn in Miss Eaker's bum. Go ahead and feel those cheeks and put a finger inside. She's well trained, now, just like Miss Eaker will be."

As Amanda watched James advance two paces toward Miss Miller's proffered backside, pink anus over pink cunny, between buttocks the girl herself must hold open, she felt her fingers of their own accord find their way inside the valley of her own bottom, touch her own bottom-hole. She remembered the way James had put the head of his cock there, and then suddenly stopped, come around the bed, and asked her to marry him.

For a moment it seemed he had eyes only for Miss Miller's bottom, and the idea of the *terrible price* came upon her: she would be a wife, but her husband wouldn't really *belong* to her, would he? He would look at the cunnies and bottoms of other young ladies, and fuck them as he liked.

Then, to her surprise, he turned and looked at her. Amanda realized that her blush had gone, and she must be pale as a sheet at the prospect of James fondling Miss Miller's bottom.

"Come here, Amanda," he said. "Let's show Mr. Stallings your backside, too. You won't be fucked there today, but a finger won't harm you. You can bend over right next to Miss Miller."

He *did* belong to her, didn't he? He hadn't simply left her there, to go touch Miss Miller's pretty bottom—and he wouldn't ever, would he? He had asked her to marry him, when he had no need at all to do so. Amanda's heart rejoiced, suddenly, despite the extremity of this strange scene. It seemed much less terrible a price to pay, now that James had summoned her to display her own anus alongside Miss Miller's.

She felt the heat in her face return as she hurried over.

Mr. Stallings chuckled. "She's blushing, Coventry. Don't worry, Miss Eaker; that's what these side-by-sides are for. You won't see Beatrix blush today, I wager."

Amanda, who had been about to bend over obediently next to Miss Miller, stopped suddenly, looking from Mr. Stallings' smiling face to James' graver one. She still had her right hand behind her, on her bottom, and she realized that she must look to James like she had decided to disobey him.

"Go ahead, darling, and show Mr. Stallings your cunt and your anus," he said sternly. "He's waiting."

Why had she stopped? Because Mr. Stallings had called attention to her blush. Because he had pointed out that Beatrix Miller hadn't blushed, but instead had obediently assumed the humiliating pose of a girl displaying her most intimate charms to a man not her husband or even her protector. Beatrix had to offer her private places to James, Amanda's fiancé, and she hadn't even blushed.

"No," Amanda said softly. To bend that way, and then to mount the terrible thing on the bed, facing Miss Miller, and then to be fucked and watch the fucking—all the fucking recommended by Dr. Brown. She couldn't, because if she did, she wouldn't blush anymore. How could she ever blush again, if she had to grant James such conjugal rights as these?

"Oho," said Mr. Stallings genially. "Does someone need a whipping? Let's whip them on the saddle! Beatrix has it coming, too, since she answered back when I told her she had to leave off reading her novel to train with Miss Eaker."

"I did not!" Miss Miller said, straightening up suddenly. Mr. Stallings, without any further warning, stepped forward and seized her around the waist, bent her down again over the bed, and began to spank her very hard. Amanda gasped.

"Girls who are showing their arseholes," he growled, all his geniality gone for the moment, "do not speak, do they?"

"Ow! Please, Henry!"

But Mr. Stallings kept spanking. Amanda felt terribly faint. What had happened?

"Do they, dearest?"

"No! No, sir! Please, no more!"

Miss Miller's gentleman had turned her backside a bright shade of pink in only a few moments. Now he fondled the cheeks he punished. "Nice and warm. Let's get you up on your saddle, my love." He looked apologetically at James. "You can have a feel once she's going, but it's important that Beatrix be made to masturbate directly after punishment, Dr. Brown says, and disciplined during that self-pleasure as well. I'm sure the same would do your girl good."

"That's quite all right," James said. He turned to Amanda. "Get upon the bed, darling. I shall whip you while you ride, as Mr. Stallings suggests."

What had happened? She had seen the look in Miss Miller's eyes as she, the obedient young lady who seemed to have submitted herself entirely to the natural rights of her protector, suddenly objected to being whipped. But the expression upon Miss Miller's face had not been defiance— or, rather, the defiance had looked out from her eyes alongside something else: something *exultant*?

Why would Dr. Brown recommend that Miss Miller have to masturbate after she was punished? It *must* have something to do with that expression, must it not?

She moved toward the bed, started to climb upon it, as a way of gaining a few moments to think, before she refused to mount the horrid thing, as she felt certain she would. On the bed, Miss Miller had thrown her left leg astride the saddle, and begun to lower herself so that the India-rubber tip of the phallus touched the pale pink inner lips of her cunny. The sight made Amanda feel faint once again.

Miss Miller gave an ambiguous little sob of pleasure and discomfort as she flexed her knees. Amanda couldn't suppress her own whimper of shame, and... *oh, no*... of, yes, arousal as she watched the little cunny receive the black thing deep inside it.

Then Mr. Stallings spoke, quite conversationally, and everything fell abruptly into place. *Everything*: indeed, it felt to Amanda somehow *more* than everything that assumed its proper position, as if the way it made her feel to submit to James lay further out, encompassed her more completely, than *every* or *all* or *entire* could describe.

"What Dr. Brown says, and I admit I couldn't understand it at first, is that Beatrix needs to know that I want her to feel pleasure, but that the only way for her to know that is if I punish her for it. Isn't that right, my love?"

Beatrix had begun to post tentatively up and down upon the phallus, which Amanda could see—though it made her cheeks burn anew—glistened with Miss Miller's cunny-wet. Little whining noises came from her throat, and when she answered Mr. Stallings her voice had the same quality as her whimpers. "Yes, sir. Oh, sir, please don't whip me."

"Nonsense, Beatrix. You know you must be whipped while you ride. You are a naughty girl who needs a firm hand."

Amanda's breath came in little pants as she watched Mr. Stallings fetch a strap that hung from the bedpost. Her eyes darted to the opposite post and saw that a second, identical strap hung there as well. She looked at James, and followed his eyes to the same place. Then she gazed into his face imploringly, knowing however, and loving to know, that she would find him implacable. Amanda, too, must be whipped as she rode.

Miss Amanda Eaker was a naughty girl, just like Miss Beatrix Miller, opposite whom Amanda now placed herself, the tip of her own rubber phallus just there, where James had fucked her so many times that first night. Miss Miller looked into Amanda's eyes with a wild, nervous happiness. Perspiration shone on her brow, and she cried out at the first crack of Mr. Stallings' strap.

Amanda had said no, when told to display herself: she was a naughty girl, and she would have to be whipped while she rode the masturbation saddle.

"Get that cunt on the phallus, Amanda," James said, putting his hand on her bottom to urge her downward. Miss Miller cried out again at the second lash from the strap, and Amanda couldn't help watching the other girl's cunny as it went up and down, up and down. The frame creaked at the motion, and now Amanda herself had gone all the way down, full of the rubber cock. She held the handlebars and pushed up, and then she cried out, too, for James had fetched the strap and begun to whip her, too.

She looked into Miss Miller's face and saw that her companion on the saddle had fixed her eyes upon Amanda's cunny. The girl's glance traveled upwards, and then her eyes met Amanda's, and to her surprise Amanda saw a little pink appear on Miss Miller's cheeks.

"I'm sorry," Beatrix whispered. "I can't help it." Then she cried out, because Mr. Stallings had whipped her again, and Amanda cried out, too, at the sting of the strap.

The saddle, just at the base of the phallus, seemed to have a protuberance Amanda hadn't noticed when looking at it. Every time she took its whole length inside her cunny, her clitoris met this knob, and she quickly understood that if she ground herself shamelessly against it, and bounced herself up and down, she felt a pleasure she didn't think she had ever yet felt.

As if to confirm this possibility, she saw Miss Miller spend, then, eyes closed and head thrown back, little breasts bouncing sweetly as through the girl's screaming climax her gentleman kept whipping her. At the sight, nearly without warning, Amanda herself spent, fucking herself all the while. She cried out, "Oh, my angel," and she didn't even blush to know that Miss Miller and Mr. Stallings knew how she worshipped her gentleman.

They kept the girls on the saddle a good deal longer. James got to fondle Miss Miller, and Mr. Stallings fondled Amanda, as they rode to their second climaxes. Fingers went into anuses, and Amanda hardly blushed at all.

The gentlemen helped the girls off the saddle and removed it from the bed. They laid the girls on their sides, still facing one another. Amanda felt her leg raised, watched Mr. Stallings raise Miss Miller's leg, and then, as James began to fuck her, exercising his natural right, she watched the other girl have her own fucking by her own gentleman.

All the other things, the other permutations recommended by the doctor, would happen. Mr. Stallings would fuck Amanda, and she would watch them both fuck Miss Miller, and then she herself would have two cocks inside her. What Mr. Stallings had said about Miss Miller's pleasure, though—how she needed to know he allowed it, but she must be punished for it—seemed embodied here in its entirety. In this posture the gentlemen could caress the girls' clitorises, and they did, making both Miss Miller and Amanda cry out as the cocks plunged into them over and over. The shame of watching another girl fucked, and knowing that she herself was watched, seemed both overcome and heightened by the pleasure.

Above all, James' hips moving against her whipped bottom, punishing her anew even as he made her feel the ecstatic enjoyment to which he, her angel, had awakened her, seemed to tell her again and again that all would be well. He would have his conjugal rights, and his natural rights, and all would be well.

THE END

Printed in Great Britain
by Amazon

45653158R00076